Fanchon,
thank you for
stopping in today. Great
to meet you.
May the words on
these pages touch
your heart in some
way.
Love,
Dawn Marie

# *The Fear of* BEING SEEN

## DAWN MARIE BAILEY

WESTBOW
PRESS®
A DIVISION OF THOMAS NELSON
& ZONDERVAN

Scriptures taken from the Holy Bible, New International Version®, NIV®. Copyright © 1973, 1978, 1984, 2011 by Biblica, Inc.™ Used by permission of Zondervan. All rights reserved worldwide. www.zondervan.com The "NIV" and "New International Version" are trademarks registered in the United States Patent and Trademark Office by Biblica, Inc.™

This book is a work of non-fiction. Unless otherwise noted, the author and the publisher make no explicit guarantees as to the accuracy of the information contained in this book and in some cases, names of people and places have been altered to protect their privacy.

WestBow Press books may be ordered through booksellers or by contacting:

WestBow Press
A Division of Thomas Nelson & Zondervan
1663 Liberty Drive
Bloomington, IN 47403
www.westbowpress.com
1 (866) 928-1240

Because of the dynamic nature of the Internet, any web addresses or links contained in this book may have changed since publication and may no longer be valid. The views expressed in this work are solely those of the author and do not necessarily reflect the views of the publisher, and the publisher hereby disclaims any responsibility for them.

Any people depicted in stock imagery provided by Thinkstock are models, and such images are being used for illustrative purposes only. Certain stock imagery © Thinkstock.

ISBN: 978-1-5127-7857-1 (sc)
ISBN: 978-1-5127-7858-8 (hc)
ISBN: 978-1-5127-7856-4 (e)

Library of Congress Control Number: 2017903835

Print information available on the last page.

WestBow Press rev. date: 03/13/2017

Dedicated to my best friend, Shannon, for her unconditional acceptance. Thank you for loving me just how I am and for the freedom to be real.

# CONTENTS

# ACKNOWLEDGMENTS

I would like to thank my family and friends for their encouragement during the writing of this book, for not giving up on me, and for not thinking I was crazy. Most of all, I would like to thank the amazing people who came into my life at just the right time to share their hearts, their lives, and their stories with me. This has inspired my goal of making this book a reality. Our lives intertwined, our stories meshed, and we shared strength coming from our unique times of trauma and tragedy. I pray for all of you choosing to read this story, as it was hard fought on many levels, containing a different ending from maybe your own or that of someone you know. Nonetheless, it is no more significant than your experience or the experiences of those you love and care about.

I appreciate your willingness and time as you read the pages ahead, hoping you find peace in the words written and an even greater peace in Him, who truly has your back ... Jesus.

# FOREWORD

Someday, someone somewhere will read a book written by me. That someday, that someone, and that somewhere will, I hope, turn into many many somedays, someones, and somewheres.

The book you are holding makes you one of those someones. The day you made the choice to read it made this your someday. No matter where you may be along your path, this book, which will take me more than twenty years to finish, is resting in your possession, and that is your somewhere.

The obstacles to your someday may look like Angel's as she finds redemption, meets herself for the first time, and begins to see herself through her Father in heavens' eyes—not her biological father's eyes.

As you read, do not lose heart. Wherever your somewhere and someday finds you, I believe in you. I am proud of you. Keep pressing on, and walk with Angel. Fight with her, and forgive with her. However this book I will write comes to pass, right now, I have faith in my heart that you will find peace along the way.

—A younger me

# Chapter 1

## George Understands

*My daughter, you're my lovely daughter. You don't know this yet, and you don't know me yet, but you will. You, Angel, will reach many in my name. I have knit you together in your mother's womb, and I know every hair on your head. I save—and always will save—every tear that falls from your beautiful blue eyes. I will weep with you and share your joy. I am here even when the enemy works to destroy you.*

George understood—the lanky monkey puppet was all arms and legs and never left her side. Nearly attached at Angel's hip, George kept her safe and made her life easier to bear with his light brown fur, beady black eyes, and long red tongue that could lick her face if she opened his mouth wide enough. This made Angel giggle.

Tucking George in softly under the covers next to her with the utmost tenderness, Angel ensured his long legs and arms were all warm and comfortable. He smelled of her, even though she didn't know what that meant. He was safe, and he was her best friend. Even as furry as her puppet monkey was, she never wanted to risk George being cold, so she checked on George throughout the night, even as she slept. This made the nightmares easier to battle. Tonight was no different. She attached George's Velcro hands around her ratty pony and his feet around her waist. She tucked his tail perfectly under the blankets, and they drifted off to sleep.

The scent of her mom's cigarettes awakened Angel from her slumber the next morning. The smoke seeped from under the gap of her closed bedroom door, silently whispering, "Wake up, Angel." Crawling out from under her warm blankets, she and George were going to try to face the day. She, out in the world, and he, in the world of Angel's bedroom. Gently, she released George's loving grasp from around her hungry belly and messy ponytail. George's arms always slipped during the night, but as long as he was still close to her as she slept, it didn't matter. Angel was happy his arms comforted her, no matter where they ended up. Angel knew she would go with her mom to the food pantry after school to receive their discount groceries. Angel dreaded the long lines, but the two of them always seemed to make it tolerable, and it gave them time to spend together. Angel was always pleased to be able to help her mom.

Walking down the hardwood stairs to the kitchen, Angel expected to find her mom finishing her coffee and gathering her things to head out the door. Surprisingly, Angel couldn't find her mom, though her scent of cigarettes lingered throughout the house. Angel suddenly realized through her still sleepy eyes that it was Friday. Losing her focus on where her mom may have been, Angel gasped and realized what Fridays should mean to her.

"Dad is supposed to pick me up today after school!" Angel exclaimed.

She was sure he would make it tonight because he hadn't seen her in what felt like forever, as Angel couldn't remember how old she was the last time, yet she never lost hope. Feeling a little better about the day, she walked back upstairs with more of a spring in her step and hope in her heart that today she would be able to see her dad. Ascending the last step, she heard whimpers and cries from her mom's bedroom door.

Knocking softly, Angel asked, "Mom, are you okay?"

"Angel, go to school. I have a headache, but I will be okay," her mom replied through the tears she tried to hide.

Turning back to her room, Angel once again felt sadness sweep over her. She did not know what she could do to help

3

her mom. She quickly sorted through her dresser of almost clean clothes and picked out her red Garfield pants and purple flowered shirt, wondering why she had even been born. She wished above all wishes that she were like the other girls. She wanted their nice clothes and friends, and she wished she felt protected. As she brushed her teeth, which were in desperate need of braces, she looked into the mirror and knew that nothing she wished meant anything. She didn't even know whose eyes she saw in the reflection staring back at her.

Walking out of the house and on to school, Angel held tight to the pocketknife she hid in her pocket just in case she needed it. Being frightened of everything was her way of life. She hoped no one would see her as she made her way into the front doors of Kingston School. Angel was fond of Mr. Martin. Admittedly, she wished he were her dad. His perfectly organized eighth grade classroom always made Angel feel as though she learned better, and Mr. Martin's way of encouraging her studies made the school day seem not so bad.

As recess drew near, Angel was excited to play basketball and hoped that no one would bother her. Before she walked to the playground, Mr. Martin tapped Angel on the shoulder and told her, "It takes more muscles to frown than to smile." Mr. Martin also had a way of making Angel's blue eyes light up. She felt he cared if she were sad. He patted her on the head and smiled as the class sprinted ahead of her, as they always did, to the playground.

Angel picked up her speed and carried the playground basketball to her favorite basketball hoop. Looking up at the rim, she wished she could be taller, stronger, and faster. Closing her eyes, she imagined making every shot during recess and being a basketball star someday. This dream didn't scare her; it only made her work harder. Hope was hard to come by, but she found it in this dream.

Angel could still see herself swishing many baskets in a Bobcat uniform. She wanted badly to never let go of this dream. Here, she felt as though she could be someone. Then, maybe her dad would notice her, and maybe the popular girls would like her and be her friend. Her dream drowned the ache and fears of her life. But like a thief attempting to steal priceless jewels, she was scared it would disappear even if she could see it so clearly that it felt like it was within her reach. As recess ended, she went off to lunch. She acknowledged that she'd made more baskets than she'd missed, so she was pleased. Angel was getting hungry.

As usual, the packed lunchroom displayed all the kids with their fancy lunchboxes and those who waited in the regular line. The kids' chatter was deafening, and the heat from the kitchen almost rested in a dense film over all the lunch ladies' heads. Sometimes, Angel wondered whether they were robots, the way they acted in unison and like a perfect assembly line, feeding all the little minions.

Angel waited until everyone was nearly through the line before she took her place with the kids who had a different color lunch ticket. It reminded her of how different she was. Angel and a few other low-income kids standing next to her had free or reduced lunches. They were always the last ones to eat and never had enough time to finish their meals or get to class.

Her school was one of the few in the area that accommodated special-needs kids. Angel always helped the teachers' aides as they served the kids in their wheelchairs at the tables near the front of the cafeteria. Their arms and legs either couldn't move or were so rigid that they couldn't move unless the nurse was performing daily range-of-motion exercises. Even as young as she was, Angel hoped someday she would be able to help people who couldn't help themselves.

After school, Angel walked home along the same path as she had that morning. She noticed the busy cars and the smell of cigars that made her neighborhood easily recognizable. The neighbor boys had screaming fights, and the neighborhood drunks always created a stir. Angel looked down at her feet, trying not to be noticed as she passed by Rick's house, shaking her head. She couldn't escape the memories of his dark, oily makeshift auto shop. As she blinked harder and harder, she could feel footsteps behind her. "Please, no!" she silently screamed as each footstep seemed to vibrate the cement beneath her feet. Where was her pocketknife? Angel didn't know why she insisted on carrying it with her, but it made her feel safe, even though she knew she couldn't do much to defend herself.

Frantically, she searched her pockets, relieved to feel it at the bottom of her right pants pocket. She held on to it as she heard Rick's raspy voice call her name. "Angel, where are you going in such a hurry?" he asked with a tone of voice that made her stomach turn.

"Home," Angel replied matter-of-factly. "My mom is waiting for me, and my dad is picking me up tonight."

Angel lied, but did everything within her childlike and naïve power to not enter Rick's garage, knowing her mom wasn't home and wouldn't be for another hour . And there was never any guarantee her dad would remember to pick her up. She hoped today would be the day it would not be a lie—that her dad would find her and tell her he loved her. She grasped the rusty pocketknife harder and opened it with one hand as it broke the skin at the palm of her hand. She didn't feel anything except small, piercing stings and the moisture lining the inside of her pants pocket.

Rick was a dirty middle-aged man who never brushed his teeth. He frequented the makeshift auto shop that he and some of his acquaintances had created in an old, oversize garage. This dilapidated garage was set back from the actual house it belonged to, and he and the others worked on cars of all shapes and sizes. However, they never fixed any of the cars, as day in and day out, they sat parked in the exact location where they had been for months. Angel always wondered why he was so interested in showing her his latest car repairs when nothing ever changed.

Walking into his garage, she found herself becoming invisible, the sting lessening at the palm of her hand, she noticed how Rick's pants never quite fit and the black stains that covered his shirt never quite came clean. The odor of his body never quite went away. Angel then noticed the yellow rings of perspiration that he carried on his T-shirts with a pit in her stomach. Everything that she couldn't explain, including these T-shirts, became all too familiar.

"Angel, you could learn to be a mechanic like me someday," Rick said in a proud voice as he took her hand in his and bent over to show her his latest engine. To Angel, maybe being a mechanic wouldn't be so bad, and as scared and intimidated as she was to be coerced into Rick's domain, she somehow and in some way felt like he gave her attention. Rick's attention made her feel important even though it hurt, because in her simple and immature mind, attention of any kind was something Angel never received anywhere else. She hadn't any proverbial yard stick to measure what normal was.

As Angel placed her hand on the hood, the grease was so slick under her feet that she fell to the ground. Desperately, she searched for her knife, but it was gone! She pushed the hair from her eyes only to smear oil from the floor onto her face. Wiping her shirt, she heard the garage door motor from above—it was closing. As she feared, Rick was closing the door again, something he always did when he brought Angel in to teach her about engines. He was convinced he could teach Angel how to be a mechanic, saying it would make her useful someday.

She had to get out of the garage, but how? She never knew, and today was no exception. The only light that showed today was barely through the walk-in door as it rested slightly ajar. At that moment, she knew was defeated once again. She tried to remember where Rick's dirty tools were hanging, wishing they would come off the walls and him as she lay there against the car that with each week never got fixed. Rick proceeded to steal more of Angel's young innocence and ultimately more pieces of her soul.

Angel's eyes opened and feeling crept back into her legs as she heard her mom yelling her name.

"Angel, come home!" Angel's mom screamed.

In disbelief that her mom was home, she questioned if she had really heard her mom's voice. *Help me, Mom,* Angel thought to herself as she created the vision in her mind of her mom crashing through Rick's garage door and rescuing her. As he told her how very pretty she was, she wriggled and wriggled to escape and move toward the bright sliver of light coming from under the door. Throwing open the door and barely able to stay on her feet, she ran as fast as he could around the corner to her home, where George was.

Angel stormed through the front door of the crowed duplex she and her mom lived in, knowing that since it was still daylight, the cockroaches wouldn't be under foot. She continued her escape to the restroom to clean her stains of shame.

"Angel, hurry up in there. Larry is coming over," her mom said with excitement in her voice. The food pantry would have to wait.

For a moment, she stopped trying to make herself clean and felt delight in her heart because Larry would be here soon. Larry was a tall and handsome man her mom was to marry. He was very smart, and Angel appreciated how he made her smile, even when he was busy. Setting the washcloth down on the toothpaste-stained sink, Angel realized the bar of soap was nearly gone, but Angel set it back on the edge of the bathtub. She slowly and cautiously opened the restroom door, gathered her dirty clothes, and briskly walked across the hall into her bedroom. She felt like the frog in the Atari game Frogger as she almost leaped into her room not to be seen and squashed by her mother's questions. Closing her door, she put different clothes on and sighed as she laid back next to George and stared into his loving eyes. Across the room, she had her bag packed in case her dad did come get her this weekend. It had rested in the same position for so long that clothes inside probably wouldn't even fit her anymore. At times, this bag almost taunted her saying that she wasn't worth anything to her dad.

Soon, Larry would arrive, and she managed to give a small smile to George. Angel loved Larry, but he wasn't her dad, though something about the way Larry acted toward her made her feel safe. He talked a lot with her about God. He enjoyed taking Angel and her mom to church, but she couldn't understand what all the singing and the reading of the Bible meant to her or for her life.

Standing up, she gave George a quick kiss, grabbed her

basketball, and took off outside to use the broken hoop attached to an abandoned garage. No one had lived in the run-down house next door for as long as Angel could remember. The sharp gravel rocks made it hard to dribble and shoot, but maybe the challenge of controlling the ball would help her be a better player. She could still see her house and would know if her dad came to pick her up, and she would know when Larry drove down the street. Larry's car gave him away—he drove a sporty stick-shift car, a Toyota MR2. Silver with shiny black tires and black leather seats, it always made a tinny sound as he raced down her street.

While practicing her layups for a short time, Angel saw Larry's sporty car and heard it race by, making one more game-winning layup. Angel headed for home with a skip to her step.

"Hi, tweetie," Larry greeted her as he stroked under her chin just to tickle her. This was his usual way of telling her hello and it made her feel special. It turned out that on this particular Friday, he had more in mind to make Angel smile. Larry was going to teach her to drive his sporty car.

"But I'm not old enough yet, Larry," Angel said regretfully.

"We will go to an empty parking lot somewhere. It will be okay. I can't have you getting your permit someday and not know how to drive a manual transmission," he replied with a smile.

Nervously, she finished her supper, placed George in her backpack, and set sail for a parking lot with Larry, knowing that wherever they were going, she would mess everything up. That's just what Angel thought she did.

Behind the wheel, she could feel at least a thousand butterflies fluttering in her stomach. If she could see them, they would be every color of the rainbow, all trying to fly in the same area of her stomach. She quietly asked them to settle down in there.

Soon, the butterflies obliged, and Larry was on his way to teaching Angel to drive a manual transmission. Between directions, she and Larry exchanged laughs and jokes as the car Angel seemingly was learning to control made trips back and forth throughout the large empty parking lot not far from home. Thankful there were not many cars toward the back of the large area of emptiness, she managed to make two laps without killing the engine. Larry looked over from the passenger seat with his strong hazel eyes, and she felt as though he was proud of her.

Angel, swallowing the unfamiliar taste of pride, grinned ear to ear in the passenger seat as they made their way back home. By that time, it was obvious to even Angel that her dad forgot her again.

George wasn't surprised, and neither was she. As Angel and George retired for the evening, she couldn't shake something Larry had told her while they were on their way home. He was talking about when he got nervous or uneasy that he would talk to Jesus and pray. He said that he prays a lot, even when things aren't uneasy and he isn't nervous.

Angel had a hard time with the idea of praying or having a relationship with Jesus, as Larry called it, with someone you couldn't even see. How could you believe that this person or spirit could hear or even care? Drifting off to sleep, her weathered basketball at the foot of her bed and the bag for her dad's still in its same place, she found that tonight in the stillness of her familiar and dark room, she began to pray as the light from her miniature television lit up a small corner of the room with the various sports scores for the week. This was something Angel tried to wait up for, always anticipating that her favorite teams would be victorious.

Unable to awaken, she couldn't leave from the dream that chose to torment her tonight. Echoes of loud voices surrounded her, sounds of her dad's footsteps, her mom's cries, a commotion of things being broken as the man who was her dad was drinking again. She tried to find the will to awaken but could see clearly herself as a young girl, running through the house trying to find her mom. She knew she was sleeping, but the dream was too powerful to break away from. The slamming front door usually meant that her dad had left her house, and Angel felt her heart pounding in her chest. Her respirations became faster. Amidst the fogginess of her dream, she found her mom bent over the kitchen table, her tear-stained silky night gown clinging to her cowered body. Angel looked around the house, still unable to open her eyes, seeing her mom's things strewn about. Dreaming but wide awake, she crawled onto her mom's lap, only to slide from her mom's silky pajamas. Unable to keep her grip, she slipped and hit the floor with a crash.

Suddenly, Angel sat up straight in bed, with her heart beating as though she had just finished a marathon. She dabbed the moisture from her forehead and hated her dream. Unable to return to sleep, she waited for the sunlight to come and the cockroaches to be gone from her floor before she got out of bed. All the while, she thought about how praying the night before had been dumb and a waste of her time.

Finally, there was daylight. She was relieved the darkness was gone, but knowing it was much too early to start a new day, she leaned over in her bed, checked on George, and reached inside her nightstand where she kept the journal her grandmother had given her many years ago before she passed away. Just holding it, she remembered the soft hands of her grandmother as she placed it upon Angel's lap, telling her to write love letters to God as well as her dreams, her hopes, and her feelings. Angel rarely opened the journal as it made her miss her grandmother and didn't think this God person cared about her. The outside cover of the journal was a light blue with fluffy clouds appearing in the back ground. There was a sketch of a bright sun shining onto a single tree, and a Bible verse was inscribed in sparkling gold writing at the bottom corner.

> "I lift my eyes to the mountains; where does my help come from? My help comes from the Lord, the maker of Heaven and Earth." (Psalm 121:1-2)

Looking back several pages, she decided to reread the words she had written that expressed her heartache. Angel sat cross-legged on her bed, and her eyes began to well up as she read the words from not long ago that never seem to change meaning.

> *"Dear God, I want to die in my sleep. I hide the pain, but it hurts my soul. Dad, where are you?"*

She turned to the next empty page and began to write with passion. She wrote about school, having no friends, Mr. Martin, and Rick and his dirty hands and dirty body. She wrote of driving a fast car with Larry and his smile and his eyes. She wrote of missing her dad and expressed her curiosity as to who Jesus is.

She asked herself why even in her dreams she couldn't

feel safe. The tears falling from Angel's eyes now hit the pillow. She closed her journal and placed it into her backpack. Even though it made Angel miss her grandmother, writing somehow helped her breakaway from life and made her happy. As she finished letting all the tears out, she got up and was going to face another day with the deep aches of fear and worthlessness defining her horizon.

# CHAPTER 2

# NUMB

*Angel, I hear your silent prayers, and I know your heart. I am Jesus. I see you, and I know the path I have for you. Your faith will grow, and you will believe though have not seen. Your Father in heaven adores you and will give you the strength and courage to accomplish the impossible.*

With summer break approaching, Angel continued to miss what she wished her dad would be. She hadn't been able to see Larry much as he was in and out with his career and often wouldn't come by their home until Angel was asleep. In fact, lately, she noticed Larry changing when he was around, acting distant and quiet.

Angel made plans for her summer days, knowing this was going to be the time she would have to prove she was good enough to play for the best coach in high school girls' basketball. Coach Patrick was a plump, intimidating fellow who expected 100 percent intensity from his players. Angel tried not to make eye contact with him during the basketball meeting that filled most of her morning today. The meeting was important and was to solidify the year ahead.

Looking at the floor, she knew to get even the slightest chance to play, she would have to outperform Nora, Katherine, and Jessica.

These three girls had flawless lives, straight As, and perfect families. She hated them, but this wasn't going to stop her. Playing basketball was the only good thing in her life. "What would these girls think if they knew I slept with my basketball?" she asked herself silently with a snicker.

As information was being given regarding summer camps, Angel could tell the girls were looking at her and exchanging conversation about her. Angel's head lowered even more as she pretended to be tying her already tied shoes. The scars were still on her hands from the rusty pocket knife. Noticing her skin scaring, her first reaction was to cross her arms at her waist. Shame surrounded her as she remembered how Rick had always made her feel pretty, but why did she feel so alone and scared? Angel began to become frustrated that these thoughts were interrupting her focus on what was happening at the meeting. The cuts proved her belief of worthlessness and hopelessness—the two friends she did get along with and who liked her. Maybe if she were a good basketball player, Rick and her friends, worthlessness and hopelessness would go away and stop being the demons that followed her around 24 hours a day 7 days a week.

She was glad when meeting finally concluded, knowing there wouldn't be enough money in her mom's budget to get her to all the camps, but she knew her mom would do everything she could to get her to be able to go to at least one of them. She would stop home quick and then begin her summer break for real.

The Kingston school playground, though nestled in a rundown neighborhood with broken houses and broken cars, was provided new basketball hoops. As Angel took her first step onto the blacktop of the playground on her first day of summer break, she wondered why on the walk to the today that she noticed Rick's house being boarded up. She further wondered why his damaged and rusty cars with no engines were gone. These became just fleeting thoughts, however, because she welcomed the feelings of thankfulness for summer break and having more time to play basketball. Admiring the secondhand store-brand shoes she hadn't quite broken in yet, she noticed how they were still bright white and a bit stiff from newness. Angel was proud of the orange shoe strings she added to look more like a Bobcat next year. The more expensive shoes all the other girls wore, though nice and expensive, couldn't compare to how hard her mom worked to buy her the basketball shoes she had on her feet.

Fantasizing that her team's bench was located on the hoop side out of the sun, she used her basketball as a seat, tied her hair into its usual ratty ponytail, and reached into her backpack for her journal. Sometimes, writing words in her journal made more sense if she were on the court. Today, she wrote about feeling distracted, about wondering if she would ever be married, and whether she would ever have children. Angel was beginning to feel the unanswered questions of what would become of her without basketball. Would this God she was supposed to pray to and worship continue to make it hard for her to breathe? Her cuts, though healing, made her feel ashamed, but she wrote of how they also somehow gave her power. Angel drew a picture of the heart she embedded just the night before into her right hip.

Raising her shirt to look at her side, she was impressed with the scar forming already over her protruding hip bone.

She ended the entry writing about how much she missed her dad, asking herself why Larry was never home, and tried to create a sentence that would make that all okay. Under her heart, she lightly sketched the name *"Jesus"*.

"Oh, no!" she exclaimed. "There are other kids coming over here."

Quickly, she stuffed her journal into her backpack. Fidgeting with the broken zipper, she finally was able to close the backpack completely. Standing up without hesitation, Angel tossed her backpack under the hoop she claimed as hers. Glaring at the other kids, she wished herself stronger than she was to keep them away from her and her basketball hoop.

Soon, she was outnumbered, and her ball was lost among everyone else's. Angel felt sucker punched. This was her hoop, and she was being pushed out. "Didn't anyone see me?" she asked as beads of sweat formed on her forehead and tears filled her eyes. She couldn't believe how much she hated her life. Grasping the torn corner of her backpack, she took off as fast as she could toward the field. She felt her body slow, and she began coughing in between tears. She sat with her back against the oak tree that arose from the center of the grassy field attached to the playground. Tilting her head back, she dared the sun for a staring contest. Losing, she waited for the black dots to go away and rested her head on her bent knees. She wondered what was wrong with her. Her heartbeat was the only thing she felt in her body. Making a fist, she stood up and faced the tall oak tree as big around as the biggest tree she has ever seen.

Throughout all the years attending Kingston School,

Angel never personally met the oak tree until today. Looking over her shoulder and around this monstrosity of a tree, she could see the other kids in their more expensive shoes and more expensive clothes shooting at her basket. Suddenly, a shot of unexpected pain went through her back as if each vertebra was going to give out and she would crumble to the ground. Angel placed her forehead against the tree, keeping both hands clenched in a fist. At this moment, she hated her mom for making her back get checked. She had scoliosis, the reason her back hurt, and sometimes, made it even harder to breathe. Angel felt as though she were at an even more disadvantage, and this reinforced her thoughts of never being able to amount to anything. The plaster back brace had been ordered; a turtle shell of sorts would soon surround her damaged body. It was just one more thing the other kids could make fun of her for. Hopefully, her mom would have enough money to buy a bigger bag that would hide her back brace when not having to wear it.

"Angel, we need you to wear this every day for at least twelve hours." Dr. Casper's voice still rang in her ears even though her appointment had been weeks ago.

Bringing her clenched right fist to her shoulder, she began get to know this tall oak tree. As the minutes passed by, Angel continued to chip away the bark, feeling no pain, and as the minutes passed by, Angel got to know this tree very well. Becoming angry, she begged and pleaded the tall oak tree for help, but it just stood there in all its glory, just towering over everything and everyone else with a presence like no other tree she would ever see or get to know would.

Getting herself together, she told the tree that never helped good-bye. With its leaves blowing ever so slightly in the breeze, the tree waved good-bye at Angel. Dragging her hand through the long blades of grass, she was thankful the people were not caught up on their mowing at her school. The blades of grass and supple flowers served as comfort as they cushioned her fists and hands. Angel managed to carry her backpack and basketball home.

As Angel walked through the door to her front porch, she was surprised how much the summer heat that collected on the enclosed porch greeted her overly warm body.

*Mom will be home soon,* she thought. Upstairs in her room, she put her basketball on her unmade bed where George kept her blankets a mess. He never liked the bed made. Not wanting anyone to find her journal, she opened her nightstand and placed it back in the drawer beneath the presidential awards she won in grade school for physical fitness, something Angel was proud of herself for.

"I love you, Grandma," she spoke as she caressed the cover of her journal, reading again the gold glittered verse on the bottom corner:

> "I lift my eyes to the mountains; where does my help come from? My help comes from the Lord, the maker of Heaven and Earth." Psalm 121:1-2

Angel dropped to her knees and fought the voices in her head telling her she was worthless and that her dad didn't love her. She fought her feelings of never being able to be a princess, and she fought remembering her mom's tear-stained silky purple pajamas. The demons of her reality were not leaving anytime soon.

The sound of the rickety porch door startled Angel. They had been needing a new door on the porch but there was never enough money.

"Jesus, I hate you," Angel said as she stared at the wounds on her fists.

Angel's mom came through the always-squeaking porch door, and by this time, Angel was in the kitchen looking for something to eat.

"Hi, Mom," Angel said. She felt guilty because she usually had the house clean before her mom got home.

Angel's mother had no idea how much her daughter was spiraling out of control. Her secret thoughts of wishing herself dead would devastate her mother if she knew.

A single mom who worked two or three jobs most of Angel's life, she a pretty lady with overwhelmingly sad eyes still full of the tears she cried the night before. Would Larry be her hero? Angel didn't know, but she longed for Larry and her mom to be together forever. Right now, however, Larry was nowhere to be found. Angel couldn't remember the last time she heard him come visit.

Angel's mom gave her a quick hug while juggling a large bag marked with her doctor's logo. Instantly, Angel acknowledged the never-ending back pain that had plagued her since birth. Angel knew that what was inside the confines of the brown and depressing satchel was her turtle shell. It was orthotic, as Dr. Casper, her orthopedic doctor explained so well.

Angel could smell her mother's machine shop on her, consisting of metal and exhaust scents that permeated the orthotic bag as her mom handed it over to her. Every time she smelled her mother's clothes, she knew how hard of a day she must have had, and it made her feel even guiltier for being grouchy about the brace. Her mom worked in a factory making small parts for bigger parts serving different companies and always came home exhausted. The heat was too much to bear in the summer, and just the opposite was true about the cold in the winter, as the factory had no thermostat.

Today, Angel would have to start the wearing schedule for her brace so it could attempt to correct the curvature of her spine, decrease her back pain, and allow air to enter and expand her lungs, as taking a deep breath never was attainable for Angel. The brace was a sterile white, and as Angel took it out of the bag, she was surprised how it shined. Four straps would attach the back together as she tightened it up just like the doctor had shown her at her first appointment. It felt as if Angel's insides were smashed together like sardines. A small light cushion lined the inside of the brace that would soon be digging into her skin. After the countless hours of it resting just over her ribs, it would contribute to heat rash. Eventually, heat rash set in, blocking Angel's pores making it impossible for the sweat from her thin body to escape. The friction from her orthotic was unforgiving. Over time, her abdomen became home to tiny bumps surrounded by red and prickly tender skin. Angel would whimper into George's trusting lanky arms begging, "Daddy, Daddy help me" until her eyes closed. She wouldn't be able to fight keeping her eyes open, and the cries for her dad would fade into emptiness.

The first week of summer wasn't what Angel had hoped for, considering there were other kids using her basketball hoop, she had a terrible case of heat rash, she had yet to see or hear from her dad, and that she fought hidden thoughts daily of why she was even born.

Walking past Rick's this particular sunny summer morning on her way to the playground, she felt her throat tighten as she saw the man with rough hands sweeping various car pieces mixed with nuts and bolts of that made a terrible scraping sound against the broom. Angel was really

23

good at taking herself out of her body, and she felt as though she were able to do things other kids would never have to do. Angel gasped for the remaining air that was trying to escape her lungs. She began to walk faster and faster, no longer hearing the traffic. The noise of the cars and loud trucks disappeared as she remembered seeing Rick's place empty and deserted not too long ago.

Without warning, Rick dropped the broom that was permanently stained from his hand prints. Angel felt much like Rick's broom must have felt—dirty, stained, and worn out. He turned around and saw Angel and started walking toward her while dodging spare tires, air compressors, and various tools that never seemed to do their job. Ultimately, he cut Angel off midstride at the sidewalk. Angel wondered how anyone could even live there, with its ram shackled windows and doors. There were broken boards all over his porch and broken windows lining the front of his house. She daydreamed of him falling through and getting injured badly from a piece of the splintered wood. Angel was proud of how she could create such a vivid scene in her mind that almost came to life the longer she thought about it.

"Angel, your hair. It has gotten so blonde and so much prettier since summer has started," Rick commented.

Rick walked behind Angel and coerced her back to his garage, where he had only said he would be a minute and then she would be free to shoot her ball.

Each second of that minute seemed like an eternity. Angel waited and thought about how much she hated her existence. The fear turned to numbness, and Angel could see herself apart from her body. She envisioned being on the starting line up wearing the Bobcat orange basketball uniform, and she could even hear the crowd cheering. Her one moment of triumph ended as quickly as it began.

"God, please kill me," Angel said as she stood with her basketball and stumbled toward the sliver of light beneath the garage door.

"Did you say something, Angel?" Rick asked in a creepy, out-of-breath voice.

"No," Angel replied with a voice that convinced her she was dead.

"Try not to miss me too much, Angel. I'm moving back to my hometown, far from here," Rick admitted.

Angel was already in a sprint toward the playground and the mighty oak tree she saw every day that summer that never seemed to help her. Angel believed that may have been the fastest she had ever run. Regrettably, she had dumped her entire water bottle along the way, trying to quench her thirst and immerse herself in cleanliness, even if it was stale water from a day ago. She set her ball down next to the school and sat on its weathered leather as she always did before she took the court. This gave her some peace by getting her thoughts in order where her focus needed to be. This was also her favorite place to rest in between bouts of shooting practice. *Just a few minutes of rest*, she thought as she tried to catch her breath. Angel began to feel an overwhelming sense of fear and panic come over her as her suffocating turtle shell made slow, deep breaths an impossibility.

Angel stood up and walked as close as she could to the brick walls of her school, skimming her hands across the hardened mortar and clay. With each slow, deliberate, and methodical step, she no longer felt the sadness and loneliness within her. Each brick served its purpose that day for Angel, and it wasn't just to erect the school building that would

25

house her educational experience. Eventually, she negotiated herself right back where she started, believing to have looked in every window she could reach as the warm bricks took away her grief. Her basketball sat patiently waiting for her return. She was no longer scared and didn't feel panic or suffocation, only pleasure that her emotional pain had gone away ... at least for the time being.

After shooting for nearly a half an hour, it was obvious to even Angel that she couldn't even reach the hoop with her jump shot or layup. Not from the hot sun, but from the discomfort she had inflicted to her hands at the bricks expense. Deciding to give up, she, one step at a time, marched home.

As she neared her porch, something inside of Angel felt off. Something didn't feel right. She noticed Larry's car parked in front. That was strange as Larry never left work early. Even when he was sick, he would still make it to work. Larry always referred to his years in the Navy, making him such a hard worker not to mention how strong he is. Angel was always in awe of Larry's physical strength.

Peeking around the corner, she saw Larry seated on the couch, smiling as if to be there only to see her. Angel smiled back, confused, though happy to see him.

Larry stood up and said, "Angel, I've got a surprise for you." Larry put his strong arms around her and kissed her head, something he'd never done, and whispered his secret surprise into her longing ears.

Hesitating, Angel questioned him. "Really?" Surprises weren't exactly a positive thing in her life.

Angel knew Larry was a pilot and owned a small airplane, but never would she have ever thought that he would have ever wanted to take her flying in his airplane. This may have been the best surprise ever in her entire life.

Larry made sure Angel's mom knew, and everything was put into place. Angel was more focused now that she noticed Larry was serious. He didn't have his usual professional clothes on, which was her first clue that this was going to happen. Being a college professor, he always had to look dressed up, making him look even more handsome. *Something else is different*, Angel thought. She knew he wasn't dressed for teaching, but there was something more she thought she observed. Taking a closer look, she saw how tightly his belt was around his waist and that his pants still looked to be too large. She understood that it had been several weeks since seeing him, but he looked different. Larry was wearing a baseball cap, which seemed awkward as she never saw him wearing a cap except in the winter. She found a way to shrug off what she noticed and maintain her excitement for flying.

"Are you ready, sweetie?" Larry asked.

"Um, yes, but can I bring George?" Angel asked a bit embarrassed by her request. She had been thinking in the past several weeks that maybe she was getting too old for George's company.

"Of course," Larry replied without hesitation.

They were soon out the door, and Angel knew George wouldn't take up much room. On the way to Larry's cabin where he had his plane, she realized it would take a little while to get there, but she didn't care.

George rested on her lap, and the highway markings passed and the clouds formed magical scenes of faraway lands. It was such perfection and beauty. Angel found herself in that moment to be happy and appreciative of how she had a gift inside of her to be able to see the small but beautiful things around her.

Larry's cabin was surrounded by a small pond that Angel loved to swim in and catch bullfrogs from. The metal and wood bridge that carried her bare feet in the summer along the other side of the pond to beat the bullfrogs into the water was her solace, her safe place. Larry's cabin was nestled in between an overgrown patch of plants covered with blackberries. On one summer day last year, Angel enjoyed wiping out the entire delicious crop. She loved to snack on them. Recognizing the fact that she hadn't been to Larry's cabin in what seemed like forever, she was very thankful for this day. Larry turned his sporty MR2 off the interstate, and they were now on the county blacktop road that led to his cabin. They were almost there.

"Angel?" Larry said her name, and it startled her.

"I have another surprise for you. It's sitting in my pole building," Larry said. "When we get to the cabin, go in and check it out." Larry spoke with anticipation and made Angel even more thankful for this day. Passing the small rural airport where Larry's plane was, she knew the next turn was Larry's driveway to his cabin and pole building.

The car came to a stop in front of the pole building where inside was yet another surprise awaiting Angel. She already felt Larry had done so much that she didn't need anything else. She fought with her seatbelt, exited the car, and ran over to the large overhead door to his pole building. She slowly lifted from the middle just like Larry had taught her on one of her visits here. Otherwise, the sides would catch, and they would have an all-day struggle to try and open it. The heavy door lifted with ease, and she had it up over her head in no

29

time. Though heavy, she gave it one more push, as hard as she could, and opened the door completely.

Angel couldn't believe her eyes. Sitting among Larry's mowers, snow blowers, and older classic cars was a red Honda three-wheeler. Its knobby wheels took Angel's breath away, and the shiny red paint was almost too pretty to look at. Larry watched Angel, and she could see how full of satisfaction he was. He wiped a tear from his eye and walked inside closer to this special moment that Angel would never forget.

Angel ran to meet Larry at the entrance of the building, throwing her arms around him and never wanted to let go. It wasn't the three-wheeler. It was the love he had shown her and the tear in his eye that made her heart full. She kept thanking and begging him to be able to ride her new three-wheeler. Larry proceeded to, in his professor-type teaching manner, instruct Angel the ins and outs of her new machine. Trying hard to remember everything, she was like kid in a candy store and couldn't wait to start.

At last, she started the engine of the three-wheeler on her own. Larry hopped in front and Angel behind him. When it came down to it, she was nervous to drive, but she didn't want Larry to know that. Larry slowly took off out of the pole building, the sound of the motor, *now that's cool* Angel said to herself in amazement, and she couldn't believe this was her moment to shine.

Taking one lap around the pond and then another, Angel's smile could likely be seen a mile away. She felt the wind in her hair and the sting of her knuckles as it hit her hands just right, still not healed from the bricks on the school. She held on tight to Larry's waist, resting her head on his back. She wanted God to take her to heaven because she already felt like she was there.

Larry turned toward the airport where his plane was tucked safely away in a protective overhang area and where other planes also rested their wings when not in flight. Angel was startled as they and the three-wheeler crossed over into the gravel as they neared the airplanes. Three-wheelers and gravel weren't always a good combination, she recalled Larry teaching her before they left his building. Shifting her hands more around Larry's stomach as the back of the three-wheeler started to lose its footing, it was harder to hang on. Her hands grazed over something protruding from Larry's stomach. It was moveable and had a small clasp on it. It felt like a plastic tube of some sort. What was this?

Bringing the three-wheeler toward the airport office, they parked. Not soon after, the owner's dog galloped over. The old yellow lab named Buddy was was always friendly and loved to see visitors, especially Angel. He was missing part of his left paw from a hunting accident, but it never slowed him down, Buddy was born a hunter and a chaser of squirrels and rabbits. He would sometimes wander over to visit Larry's cabin and spend the day.

Buddy and the new three-wheeler couldn't shake the curiosity in Angel's mind of what was the tube hanging from Larry's stomach. Why was it there? What did it do?

Larry handed Angel the key to the three-wheeler and said she would be driving back. She closed her hand tightly and confidently said, "Okay."

Walking closer to the airplane that Larry said would make her feel closer to Jesus, she placed both her scarred hands and wrists onto the smooth covering of this large object that would lift her and George into the air.

"Oh, wait, Larry! I forgot George!" Angel panicked.

Larry, not shaken, told Angel it was okay, reminding her that he had given her the key.

"Go on and get George. I will wait here for you guys," Larry said.

Angel proudly placed the key into the ignition of her shiny new machine. The black seat was warm from the sun, but that didn't matter. She couldn't believe this motorized beauty was all hers. As Larry instructed, she gently accelerated using her right thumb on the gas and her left foot at the gears. That's one thing Angel found odd, that three-wheelers were designed at times with the throttle near the right thumb to control instead of how motorcycles were. She supposed it didn't matter as long it as she could make her three-wheeler speed up.

Chugging away in first gear, Angel slowly moved her mighty red machine forward. Looking back, she saw Buddy run to the edge of the overhang and watch her speed away. Shifting her sights toward Larry, she witnessed him stumble and trip. If not for his outstretched arms on the airplane, he would have fallen hard onto the rough ground. Angel picked up speed, shifting to second gear. Now in third gear, she was rounding the pond next to Larry's cabin. She could see the metal suspension bridge swaying ever so softly in the breeze. The bull frogs jumped into the clear pond water one by one as the sound of the engine startled them. Those bull frogs would be really hard to catch on this thing. Her hair met the wind, and it felt good. She was free and warm, and for those moments, she didn't feel her back hurt. She could ignore the tightness of her turtle brace. Shifting the gears down so she could slow her speed and come to a stop, she spotted Larry's car still parked in the driveway. She perfectly stopped her gas-powered horse and climbed off to get George out of Larry's car.

Grabbing her lanky friend, Angel was in a hurry to get going. The idea of flying close to Jesus was so exciting. If she could talk to Him, she would ask Him to have her dad call her or come see her. Maybe if she prayed to Jesus in person instead of out the window of her bedroom or on the pages of her grandmother's journal, it would make Him listen and make Him answer. Even more so, she wanted to get back to Larry. She was worried. He looked weak today, and he stumbled nearly falling. Beyond the scars on her hands, she still felt the tube that led to the inside of Larry's abdomen.

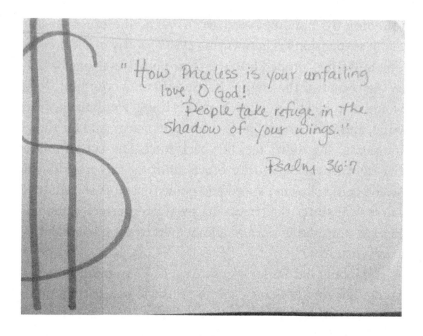

"How Priceless is your unfailing love, O God!
People take refuge in the shadow of your wings."

Psalm 36:7

She could see Buddy prancing around in the distance near the airport office door. Inside the air-conditioned airport office was a coin-operated candy machine with various types of candy and bubble gum. Buddy liked these treats, and Angel would sneak a few to her four-legged friend every chance she could. Though she never flew with Larry, she was familiar with Jane and Max, the owners of this small but popular airport tucked away near the city. If Angel and her mom were visiting, Larry would occasionally check on his plane, and Angel went with just to see Buddy.

"Are you ready, Angel?" Larry asked as he smiled.

Mr. Martin's smile couldn't even compare to Larry's today. He was focused on taking Angel up in his plane and was acting differently from how she had ever seen him act. He was tearful yet relaxed.

Angel secured her three-wheeler, stuffed George under her shirt, and tucked his arms and legs behind her back.

"Yes, let's go," Angel replied.

She was scared but hid it well. Larry instructed Angel in such a particular and specific way about the safety of the aircraft that was about to carry her into the air. She sat in the seat of this two-seated bird in complete disbelief—disbelief that someone would include her in such a majestic experience and disbelief that maybe she would see the face of Jesus. Larry continued to point out this control and that control, but Angel just stared at the never-ending vision of clouds. She swore she could see a princess in the clouds with her long beautiful hair and the laced edges of her dress. Looking even deeper, she saw a cloud in the perfect shape of a prince reaching out his hand for his princess.

Angel still heard Larry's voice educating her about the metal construction of aluminum alloy and the wing span of the airplane. She recalled how smooth and metal-like the airplane felt. The wings reminded her of Michael Jordan, the way he could dunk from the free throw line. Angel felt safe with Larry.

Making their ascent from the runway, Larry explained the fixed tricycle gears that helped land the plane and are the easiest set up for taking off. Soon, the plane's nose was in the air, and the rush was effortless. Could this be happening to Angel?

Angel believed at that moment in time she heard Jesus. She felt Him say that He loved her. Looking upon the clouds again, this time clearly beneath her, she undeniably witnessed soft and woolly looking visions that so carefully and methodically arranged themselves in the shape of a lamb. These were not like a lamb you would see in books, movies, or fairy tales, but one that was tired, sad, and could barely lift its head. In an instant, Angel felt a peace she's only dreamed of. For the first time in her life, she didn't feel alone. Larry was right—she felt closer to Jesus, and in Angel's heart, she had met Jesus for the first time.

Angel, even with her new special friend, felt a pull in her heart, a slight but ever present fear that she couldn't explain. She trusted Larry at the controls as they began their descent back to earth after a magical time in the air, but why did she feel so scared? Closing her eyes, she could visualize danger and darkness.

Landing the aluminum bird without as much as a bump, they were safe again on the ground. Angel let out a sigh and realized she hadn't spoken since meeting Jesus. Larry was grateful of Angel's appreciation and all the thank yous she showered him, but they made it even harder for Larry, who would one day very soon have to tell her that he was dying.

# Chapter 3

# The Enemy

*My daughter, you have seen my face. I am holding your heart and will never let go, I will always show you perfect love, honesty, and sincerity. The darkness you felt through the peace is the enemy who brings evil and deception to lead humanity astray. He is a liar who desires to wage war on all those who obey my Father's commandments. He rules the demons and will continue his fight until the end. Your race has begun.*

Angel continued her sun-up-to-sun-down visits to the Kingston basketball hoops. Orientation to high school was intimidating, but she just wanted to play basketball. However, tennis was a close second to what piqued her interest in athletics. This seemed to be on her mind for something else to try to succeed in. She began shooting baskets this summer morning, thinking about trying out for tennis as she remembered the tennis coach, who would also be her PE teacher, sitting at a table during orientation trying to recruit her and other girls to play for the Bobcats.

With each basket she made, the sun grew hotter. There was no breeze, which made it more difficult to stay cool. Reaching for her water bottle, she realized she had already finished her water. Packing up her things, she dribbled her ball down the street toward her empty home.

The time she had spent flying with Larry seemed like so long ago, and the conversation she recently overheard between her mom and Larry was haunting her. They weren't really in an argument, but they were discussing something very sad and intense. Angel, as she ascended her porch steps, basketball in hand, flung open the door with her foot. Her full hands made her glad the door was broken, even though it never latched and kept her awake when storms came as it banged violently into the house.

These stormy evenings were overshadowed by those late summer evenings as the lullaby the locusts made from the tree from outside her bedroom window. Those summer creatures and their unique sounds became her refuge and her place of familiarity.

Exhausted, Angel plopped on the sofa with a glass of sun tea. She always enjoyed the sun tea her mom somehow found the time to make. It helped her cool down and quench her thirst. Leaning over to untie her shoes, she saw, still at the bottom of the stairs, the bag ready to go with her to her dad's if he ever would come and pick her up. Lowering her already sullen shoulders to overcome how bad it felt that her dad never came this weekend, she found that the deep ache was beyond relentless.

She wondered if he would even know what she looked like. Angel couldn't fight back the first tear began filling her eyes. She tried to not let them fall, but in an instant, they bit her face as they mixed with the beads of sweat from shooting baskets all day.

Night was near, and Angel dragged herself to her room after doing the dishes, vacuuming, and straightening up her mom's shoes that were still soiled from her day at the machine shop. Angel always tried to please her mom and have her come home to a clean house.

Gathering her clothes, she traipsed her way to the restroom for a much needed shower. Unstrapping her back brace, Velcro piece by Velcro piece, she saw that the heat rash was now spreading to her stomach. The itching and discomfort was relentless as she took the rest of her clothes off. She noticed how her body was changing and didn't understand what it all meant. She was thankful some of her scars were healing, but she never lost the desire to make new ones.

Before falling asleep, she took out her journal and began writing about why she hadn't seen Larry since they flew in his airplane and wondering how Buddy was doing without the bits of candy she would sneak to him. Angel described how she wished she were someone else. Why did all of her tears have to sting so badly? Angel hated herself, and on that last thought, she asked Jesus to help her sleep ... just for one night.

41

Throughout the night, Angel tossed and turned with nightmares. She was haunted with dark memories she couldn't free herself from. Gasping, she sat up in bed, held onto her chest and neck, and begged for her heart to just stop beating. Why would God even give her a heart if it hurt so badly? Her dream felt so real. She was fully awake, although how could it be that her heart could pound so hard and fast that she could still be breathing. Her body felt uneasy and uncomfortable. It was then that she realized she had wet the bed. Angel rolled herself into the smallest ball she could possibly create and screamed into her pillow, feeling her own urine seep farther into her clothes, sheets, and skin.

Slinking to the laundry room, she didn't want her mom to hear her or know that she wet her bed and was still a baby. The sunrise was bright, and Angel was disappointed that she couldn't see the beauty in this morning's sunrise. It hurt her swollen eyes. Angel wanted to die again today. As she put her blankets and George into the washer, she took a screwdriver that in Angel's mind was placed there on top of the dryer for her to use to mark on her body what she deserved. It was what would ease the battle in her heart. It was lined with small enough edges, but with powerful force, it was just enough to prove to this young lady that these roaches had nothing on her. She watched them scatter on the basement floor in fear away from to reach whatever their safety was.

She added a few other dirty clothes from the floor to make a full load as her mom had always shown her.

Angel hadn't noticed her stomach growling until now. She hadn't eaten anything in more than twenty-four hours, but she didn't want to eat. Angel had come up with a way she could die. As quietly as she could, she found her way to her room. She put on her shoes, kicked her back brace under the bed, and made it outside without her mom stirring.

Angel climbed on her bike after fixing the chain that never stayed on. Her hands full of grease, she was on her way to Edgewood Road, one of the busiest of roads traveled, especially this time of day.

Angel was going to make sure to get hit by a car. Pedaling as fast as she could, she faced the traffic head on. Horns were honking, people were yelling at her, their voices were muted, and she couldn't even feel her legs getting tired. Block after block, Angel pedaled harder and faster. Seeing cars swerving, she begged for one of them to hit her. She became mesmerized with each revolution of the tires, going so fast that she couldn't even see the spokes within her wheels. Suddenly, without warning, her chain fell off. She lost control of her bike, sliding into a curb and hitting her back with great force on the cement. Angel's bike lay there in a heap, scratches and blood mixed with rocks, unsure what was bleeding and what wasn't. She could only see the gravel so meticulously embedded in her skin.

Angel was still alive, and this made her angry. She was angry enough that she pulled her bike out of its heap off the curb and picked it up with a strength she didn't know she had. From up above her head, she threw the tangled mess of once was her bike as hard as she could to the curb that was supposed to end her life. Traffic had slowed, but no one stopped. With each passing block on her way home, her bike wouldn't roll anymore as the rims were bent. She knew that she had ruined her bike forever. That was the death in this scenario—it was not her own. She felt the guilt of taking her thoughts of wanting to die out on her bike. All her bike ever tried to do was help her escape and allow her to feel free, even for a short time.

With regret, she gingerly and cowardly rested her bike against some bushes and continued her walk of shame home. Angel began to cry at the intense pain in her back, knowing she would need to ignore it no matter how painful it became, because she didn't want to lose a day of shooting baskets.

Eventually, she made it home. Her mom was gone for another day and night with her two jobs. Swallowing two Tylenol, Angel ate some crackers and had a glass of sun tea as she filled a water bottle and headed for the court.

She didn't notice the scrapes and irritation of her bike "accident" because as soon as she started shooting baskets, all the discomfort subsided. An hour or two passed when she noticed someone pulling into the parking lot. No one ever drove here to play, she told herself, especially someone driving this make and model of a car. It looked and sounded to be that of a hot rod. She stood in amazement of how nice of a car it was. It must have been worth stopping her play, because she stood in center court squinting against the sun, her basketball at her hip, admiring the shiny black IROC with a T-top.

"Wow," Angel gasped out loud.

She could even hear the exhaust as this mystery car pulled in and parked, thinking it must be fast as well. Out of the car came a man whom Angel thought she recognized from somewhere. The sun was beating down on his car, making it difficult to see who was walking toward her. It looked as though he were carrying a football and flag football equipment. *I wonder if he is meeting people here for a flag football game.* Angel thought. She was hoping they wouldn't use the hoop she has claimed to be her own. As the man approached, she now remembered him being the tennis coach and PE teacher from orientation, Mr. Hammon.

"Hi," Mr. Hammon greeted her.

"Hello," Angel replied.

The scent of the cologne he was wearing was overtaking her, almost making her sneeze, and her lungs tightened up. His tight light blue gym shorts made it obvious he was in fact a PE teacher. Angel wondered what he was doing here.

Smiling, Mr. Hammon knocked the ball from Angel's hip, grazing her side with his hand.

"Let's play one on one!" he suggested.

Angel found herself to be a little irritated, but she enjoyed the attention. It was really cool and made her feel good that someone wanted to play basketball with her, especially her future PE teacher and maybe coach if she did in fact try out for tennis. He probably knew a lot about sports and could teach her a few basketball moves that would help her in high school.

Mr. Hammon made Angel nervous. She didn't want to do anything wrong, and she worried it may affect her grade. He was a shorter man who was muscular with blonde hair, blue eyes and kept a slightly unshaven face. His smell was a mixture of cologne and soda pop, saturating the air around her.

As their game of one on one finished up, Angel felt a sense of feeling good about herself that she, much shorter, much less strong, and much less quick, kept up with him. With her last shot bouncing just off the rim and missing her opportunity to win, Mr. Hammon made his last shot, beating her score and taking the game. Angel just kept thinking how special she must be to have the teacher shoot with her and spend time with her.

"Good game, Angel," Mr. Hammon said as he rubbed her back and brushed a few strands of hair from her eyes.

"Thanks," she replied.

"I brought some flag football equipment. If you'd like, we could toss the football around," Mr. Hammon suggested.

Angel was taken aback, trying to comprehend why someone, especially a teacher, would want to spend time with her. Angel recalled their brief meeting at orientation. She remembered telling him where she spent most of her time during the summer and that she wanted to be the best athlete for the Bobcats when she reached high school.

She closed her eyes briefly and could still see the smile he gave her when telling him how hard she was going to work. Trying to get him to see why going out for tennis may not be what she wanted to do, as it would take away time she could be training for basketball.

Gathering the flags, which were hooked to bright yellow belts and the football, they swiftly walked toward the field. Nearing the large oak tree, they set their things down. Angel took the last sip of water from her NBA water bottle, embarrassed as it was worn off. Needless to say, it didn't matter to Angel. She would always be a Bulls fan, with or without a legible Bulls water bottle.

Mr. Hammon commented that his favorite team was the same as hers, though he wasn't sure who his favorite player was. He just said he liked the entire team. During their NBA conversation, Mr. Hammon asked Angel to turn around and that he would help her put her color flags on. His hands wrapped around her waist as he seemed to be having difficulty with securing the belt around her. Angel didn't believe she needed help to attach a simple belt and its flags, though maybe these were different from the kind she has used in PE class. Angel was thankful she kicked her back brace under the bed and didn't wear it here. She didn't know she would get to play sports with a coach and definitely didn't want that to be in her way. Finally, after longer than it should have taken, Mr. Hammon finally figured out how to attach the belt correctly.

"You are so thin and pretty," he said as he kept smoothing down the plastic flags.

Angel thought the flags were fine in the first place. Taking her water bottle, she tossed it against the oak tree, remembering that she took the last drink a bit ago. As it hit the strong bark of the tree, she now understood a little better why her water bottle was on its last leg.

"I have to go soon and clean my house before my mom gets home," Angel said, trying to catch her breath from outrunning Mr. Hammon during one of the last plays.

"One more hike to me," Mr. Hammon pleaded.

Squatting down, Angel tried to imagine herself a real-life center lining up in offensive position. She mustn't let him run past her. Mr. Hammon placed his hands under her stance, and for those several moments, she thought she felt him brush against her with his hand resting for his count down. Reaching down, he tripped Angel with his arm. They both landed in the grass, laughing and still out of breath from the last play.

His face was close to Angel's, and she felt his sweat drip onto her forehead. Mr. Hammon rose up onto his elbow and looked down at her. The sun was blurring her vision and made it so that she could barely look up and see the branches of the mighty oak tree that never helped but that she had gotten to know so well. His sweat stinging her eyes. He continued to tell her how in shape she was and how he could feel how strong and fast her heart was beating. His drips of sweat made their way to the corner of her mouth. In a methodical motion, he wiped his sweat from her face. Angel slithered out from under him, knowing she had to get home and get her house clean before her mom came home from work.

"Let me take you home," Mr. Hammon suggested.

Angel hesitated and gave it a second thought, but why would she want to pass on riding in such a cool car?

"Okay!" Angel said.

Making their way toward the black hot rod car, Angel was even more impressed with how it shined. What was even more unbelievable was that she was going to get to have a ride this immaculate car. The black paint sparkled, and the rims on the tires were a perfectly polished chrome. Angel hoped she would have a black car with cool rims someday.

Instead of babies and dresses, Angel had quite the Matchbox car collection she was proud of, and she loved how detailed they were. Most of her collection contained sports cars, semis, and tractors, with an occasional pick-up truck mixed in. Angel spent a lot of her time growing up organizing and reorganizing the cars and random other vehicles she collected. In fact, it's what, along with a bug buzzing around her mom's face, kept them from dying on a cold February night. Angel recalled that horrible evening as she walked around Mr. Hammon's car. She wasn't sure what triggered the memory of when the carbon monoxide infiltrated their home through the newly repaired furnace, nearly killing her and her mom. The Matchbox car she was clinging onto so desperately as the EMS personnel carried her into the hospital as she vomited the poison out of her body that night was a sports car resembling the one she was about to get to have a ride in.

She wondered from time to time if she hadn't loved Matchbox cars so much would she and her mother be dead.

Leaning into look at the inside of Mr. Hammon's car, the smell that marked him was even stronger near his steering wheel. The scent of his cologne permeated the entire interior of the car, Angel became frustrated that stupid things like her Matchbox cars and carbon monoxide from the furnace had to creep into her mind. All she wanted to do was have a fun ride home in Mr. Hammon's stylish car.

Mr. Hammon leaned up behind Angel as she peered into the passenger side window. She felt his legs on the back of hers and felt him press into her lower back. Angel wanted to open the door, but she didn't have any room to get to the door handle. She worried now that she would be too dirty from her day to be allowed to get into his car.

Mr. Hammon opened the door for her and politely invited Angel to get in. The engine rumbled, and the exhaust made the car vibrate with its powerful engine. Soon, they were pulling out of the parking lot, and Angel nervously gave him the directions to her house. She couldn't believe that this nice man was spending so much time with her. She was not looking forward to him seeing her neighborhood or house as she was sure her neighborhood wasn't like the other girls' neighborhoods from her school.

Mr. Hammon, aware Angel's NBA bottle was empty, turned into the nearest gas station.

"I'm going to get you something else to drink," he said as he positioned his IROC carefully away from other drivers already parked.

He took his water bottle inside the gas station. Angel noticed it immediately in the center counsel as she sat in the car. Mr. Hammon had one of the newer ones, lined with a material to keep the beverage fresh and colder longer. Not taking but a few minutes, he returned and handed the ice water to Angel. The time he was gone seemed to fly by, she thought, disappointed she didn't seem to have enough time to admire the controls of Mr. Hammon's car—the black of the dashboard, the feel of the leather seats still steaming hot from the sun, and the way the aftermarket radio was placed just to the right of the speedometer. Angel remembered seeing one of these in Rick's cars, though his radios never worked.

"You can have this—take it home with you," he said as Angel accepted the new to her water bottle.

Angel hesitated, even knowing how desperately she needed a new one. As she bent her forward to take a drink, she felt Mr. Hammon starring at her. His eyes were piercing. This made her choke on the sip of ice cold water as she tried to swallow. She coughed and felt more than ungraceful as she placed the bottle back in the cup holder, and in doing so, she noticed the straw that had obviously made its home in this water bottle for some time was filthy. Angel didn't want to be rude so she was able to clear her throat and take another drink. She didn't want to do anything to jeopardize him spending time with her.

# Chapter 4

## Larry

*Daughter, your earthy father has not protected you. He has not told you your worth. You know no heroes in your life. I weep at the pain others' sins have affected you and will affect you. Satan is real and in full force as you reach down to try and erase your pain. You cut your body, you scream into your pillow, you hope to die. He wants to take you from me. Someday, child, you will know that I have conquered death and sin and the enemy can't have you. He won't take you from my safe, loving, never-changing unconditional loving arms.*

Angel had no idea there would be more and more drinks from that water bottle she would partake in during the last weeks and days of summer. Mr. Hammon saw Angel nearly every day, showing up at the playground with football things and tennis things, and he always had fresh water. Angel felt good around him; in fact, she hoped he was her boyfriend. "No one had to know," he would tell her, though he never said she was his girlfriend, she knew and believed this had to be true.

Angel spent a lot of her time, if not all of her time, talking to the oak tree. Squinting her eyes against the sun at his beautiful branches, she stretched her arms as far as she could away from her body, and with her fingertips, she could touch the bark nearest to the ground. Mr. Hammon began to hurt her again. She wished she couldn't feel what was happening. Usually, Angel could draw outside her body, but it was going to take longer this time. Her face was being smothered by his sweat-filled facial hair, like daggers on their way to destroying her future. Angel kept repeating in her mind *tree, tree, tree*. Now, she felt safe. She was among the leaves, blowing in the gentle breeze. Patiently, she waited and arose from the blades of grass with another stain on her deteriorating soul.

Knowing Larry was coming over tonight, she wanted to get home. Mr. Hammon didn't offer to take her home today, but that was okay, as long as Angel knew he could still be her boyfriend. She felt loved and wanted, and this became her nutrients.

School would start in two days, and she was worried she wouldn't get to see her boyfriend as much. Mr. Hammon already told her things were going to become busier as school started, but he would see her in class. He promised he would do his best to continue to see her as the school year progressed.

Angel prepared for this because that's all he had been saying. They never really played basketball or flag football toward the end of the summer. He only would do things to her, and she made good friends with her oak tree that never helped with anything. Angel often thought to ask why he brought his basketball and flag football things if they weren't going to play anymore.

She didn't want to make him upset, so she never asked. By the end of summer, even her car rides ended. However, throughout the fal, he would occasionally make it to see her at the playground on nice days, using her body to comfort his. Angel also feared he would give her a bad grade so she just made up her mind that she would try to do what he said in class and not tell anyone what was going on or that she had this secret boyfriend.

Running up the stairs to the restroom became a pattern after Mr. Hammon dropped her off at home. Following another day at the playground, she couldn't wait to take a shower. There were areas upon her body that hurt, although her mind told her it was the way it was supposed to be. Angel let her tears be the healing rain that was ointment to the places that were exposed and vulnerable. Retching into the toilet, she could smell Mr. Hammon's cologne throughout every strand of her hair as it hung from her head, skimming the vomit-filled toilet bowl. It was a smell she could never get accustomed to—only accept. Her body reacted, and Angel did her best to soothe its pain.

Stepping into the shower, Angel took the razor before washing her violated body and created, in her mind, priceless artwork. It was at these moments that she was in control. She hoped there would be enough hot water and enough time to wash her shame down the drain. Too soon, she felt the warm water turning ice cold as it flowed over her body that deserved to die, sending chills up her spine.

Angel dressed quickly after showering. She didn't want to look at such disgrace any longer than she had to in what she was and who she was.

A light jacket would cover her newest artwork so her mom wouldn't see. Slowly, she crept down the stairs, not expecting what she would see as she descended one step at a time the closer to her living room. First, she saw the couch opened into a bed, with bags, medical supplies, nurses, and her mom with her head in her hands leaning over whatever or whomever was on the couch she never knew could open into a bed. A few nurses were moving items around the living room. She saw a wheelchair and a commode and noticed several of the things in her living room were rearranged.

She had a clear view now and dropped to her knees when she saw a man on the bed.

This man was Larry.

"Larry!" Angel cried out helplessly.

Angel found the strength to get back to her feet. Her mom quickly wiped away her own tears and rushed to Angel, holding her tightly. Angel began to cry uncontrollably.

"Mom, what's going on?" Angel asked between her tears.

As nurses continued to shuffle in and out of the house,

Angel saw one nurse unpack Larry's clothes and set them neatly folded on the end table next to the couch that was now a bed.

Angel could barely hear her mom as she felt a sudden panic engulf the room. Larry all but disappeared from her life, and it was because he was dying.

Numbness took hold, and she saw memories take shape in her brain much like a photoshoot, picture after picture. Each memory came and went so quickly and vividly that Angel nearly had trouble not fainting from the overwhelming intensity and clarity of what she was visualizing. The three-wheeler she had driven once, flying next to heaven, seeing Jesus, seeing Larry smile, feeling the tube in Larry's stomach, and watching him stumble and nearly fall. One by one, in no specific order, including the oak tree that never helped and all that ensued there, the photos were like quick flashes of light forming a nightmare of the last time she saw Larry healthy and the last time she saw anything lovely.

Angel's mom explained that Larry was having trouble swallowing. The tube leading to his stomach gave him the nutrients he needed to survive. Angel walked slowly to the bed that pulled from their couch and sat gently on the edge so not to disturb this man who was stolen by cancer. His strong body was now weak and frail, his smile was no longer bright, his eyes were now sullen, and his salt-and-pepper hair was replaced with barely a dusting of viable hair follicles. Tears streamed down Angel's face as Larry found the energy to roll toward her, his own tears soaking the pillow beneath his weary head.

"Oh, Angel," Larry whispered. "I'm sorry I didn't tell you. I thought I could get better, but I wasn't able to."

DAWN MARIE BAILEY

Angel leaned onto Larry's shoulder as he wrapped his now-bony arms around her.

"Your mom is going to take care of me. You and she are all I have". Larry trailed off into a deep sleep as he finished trying to explain how this cancer had overtaken his body so quickly. Angel stormed up to her room and threw herself into bed. She reached for her journal and reread her about the airplane and the three-wheeler. She wanted those moments to live forever, knowing that Larry would not.

56

# CHAPTER 5

# ANGEL, THE ALL-STAR

*Sweet Angel, Larry will come home to my kingdom very soon. I know you can't see me or feel my presence, but I'm here. I'm right here next to you as you sit holding your journal, now on the edge of your bed. I am embracing you. Be still. You will feel my presence, and you will hear my voice. Our enemy uses evil that is put upon us, pain and tragedy to destroy my children. When the dark one can make ashes, I have the power to make beautiful. You are blind to your own beauty. I know you will see yourself through my eyes someday.*

Opening to the next unwritten page of her journal, Angel began to write. She felt an unexpected warmth around her shoulders and at the back of her neck. Her tears stopped. Angel looked behind her and saw only her white wall with peeling paint and the familiar scratches she accidently always seemed to put into the wall anytime she rearranged her room.

On the subsequent pages, Angel planned her suicide. She couldn't take her life anymore. She was out of hope, full of emptiness. Remembering the day Larry moved in, one of the items that came, along with his mother's fine china and antique cedar chest, was a gun cabinet. She had seen the key hanging from the lock when Larry's friends carried it in.

Angel planned to sneak after everyone was asleep and take a gun, place it over her heart, and pull the trigger. She wanted to end her misery and save everyone the burden of having her around.

*I should be shot,* Angel wrote behind her descriptive sentences on how she was going to accomplish the deed. Angel wondered why Jesus wasn't helping her. Angel felt invisible with each word she wrote. With everything she had, she did her best to write how it felt to miss her dad so desperately, knowing without a doubt he didn't love her.

*"...no one will ever love me."*

She went on to write a lot about Mr. Hammon and how he made her feel, special and important. It was worth feeling the pain her body succumbed to and the shame that rained over her when he had the time to find her at the playground. Angel wrote a short prayer before closing her journal.

> *Jesus, I know you don't have time for me, but please help Larry get better. I don't want to see my mom sad, and Jesus, please let me die. Ask my dad someday why he didn't love me or want me ... thank you, Angel*

It was almost midnight, another worst day of her life. Angel quietly began her journey to the basement to where she saw the gun cabinet. Larry was asleep on the couch that turned into a bed, and her mom was keeping watch in the chair next to him, notably exhausted and sleeping ever so peacefully. Angel stopped and gazed at them both and couldn't bear to ever see that scene again. The sadness and despair that had her by the neck reinforced why she had to do what she had to do.

She opened the basement door as quietly as she could. Her house was dark, but Angel knew her way around easily, although climbing over the mountain of dirty clothes was a challenge. She made it to the pull-string light from the ceiling to turn the light on. Light entered the room, and Angel was face-to-face with ending her life.

A few steps ahead was the gun cabinet. She reached forward and placed her hands on the gun cabinet. Her curiosity was winning. The cabinet was black, rough in texture, and almost as tall as she was. Protruding and tempting her was the small key pointing right out of the lock in Angel's direction. She touched the key and then felt again the texture of the cabinet. Placing her back against it, she felt her knees give out as she slid with her back scraping down the rough surface of the gun cabinet to the moist cement of the basement floor. The drain next to the washer never drained completely.

Angel slammed the back of her head against the cabinet. She believed her life to be over. Basketball didn't matter to her, and nothing mattered to her anymore. Picking herself up, she reached out her trembling numb hand toward the small metal key. The light was just right to illuminate the self-mutilation she placed upon her wrists and arms the weeks prior.

Angel began to turn the key, hoping she could figure out how to operate the guns. She would need only one bullet. Angel knew Larry liked to hunt, so there had to be bullets—there just had to be. Turning the key to the right, it wouldn't budge. She turned to the left, and again, it wouldn't budge. Angel grew frustrated and hastily turned left and right, left and right for what felt like a hundred times, as if time were of the essence. As she screamed inside her mind furiously, she made one last attempt to open the lock. Without warning, the key broke off with a snap. In her clenched fist, she held onto what was left of the key saved her life.

During the next few weeks, Larry was slowly passing away before her eyes. Angel continued to help her mom with his care. She provided Larry with his supplemental feedings, would hold his hand, and clean his face.

The morphine was all that kept his pain away until the day he didn't wake up. Angel slept in the living room that night to be near her mom, who never stopped crying. She awakened to the sound of her voice whispering to Larry.

"It's okay, Larry. You can go home," she faintly spoke.

He passed away on the day of one of the most crucial of Angel's basketball game for the Bobcats. All her two-a-day practices led up to this moment, all the hard work against all odds this God out there certainly was looking down on her and hopefully was smiling. She was thankful during these days that Mr. Hammon took it easy on her during PE, always telling her that he wished he could watch her change clothes in the locker room. It was wonderful to Angel how pretty and important she felt when he told her these things.

Things weren't the same with Mr. Hammon though as she noticed in not too long of a time he was always talking to other girls and that hadn't spent any time with her. This made her more than aware that maybe he wasn't her boyfriend after all. If she would be more pretty or had a different body, been more like the other girls, or had clothes that were from the mall and not secondhand store, he would still choose her. Angel still had dreams and felt his body hurting hers. How her nauseated stomach became was common place when they were together. Maybe he never even loved her at all. Right now, and from now on, none of that needed to contaminate her mind.

"For the Bobcats, at guard, five six, freshman Angel Jordan." The announcer called her name.

As she ran through the tunnel of her teammates toward center court to meet her opponent, she appreciated this moment so much. The Bobcat announcer was a legend at the school, and he just introduced her, a Bobcat!

Angel felt as though she were moving in slow motion, even as the crowd cheered. As her basketball squeaked that familiar squeak, her dream was coming true in this brightly lit gymnasium, proudly illuminating the colors orange and yellow for the Bobcats. Angel had made it, she was proud of herself, and she was happy.

Every point she scored was her fuel, her food, her water, and her fight to keep going. All her pain, fear, and loneliness would flee the moment she took the court. As her feet met the hardwood, she found her freedom.

Holding onto an undefeated season being the Bobcats were about to become conference champions and would play in the State Tournament. Angel used what the deep passion from within parts of her she didn't know existed as motivation to play even harder and to do whatever it takes to win.

The game began just as they all did with the Bobcats taking the lead. Coach Patrick's trademark fast break outlet pass was flawless by this point in their season. The players knew where their teammates were going to be and when, making it impossible for the opposing teams to stop them. The crowd noise became Angel's drug.

Angel was the closest in position to become the corner outlet for the next fast break. She sprinted down the court as fast as she could. If she didn't get there in time, she would be sitting on the bench. She made it! Planting her foot, she was ready to receive the pass and get the ball into the post player for an easy two points. As she planted her right foot exactly like she had down 1,000 times during practices, she felt an excruciating pain in her right knee and dropped violently to the floor, watching her post player, Amy make the basket. Angel had another assist to add to her stats, but was it worth the cost? Sweat poured down her face as she scrambled to get to her feet. She couldn't stand, and each time she tried, Angel found herself on her hands and knees with her right knee, unable to lift off the ground. The silence in the gym was deafening. The trainer was making his way over to her, but she wasn't going to admit she was hurt. Wiping off her brow full of sweat, she saw Coach Patrick himself jogging onto the court, coming to her aid. Coach never came onto the court for an injury. Angel feared this could be bad and wished she would wake up from this terrible dream. Knowing she was awake, she clenched her fists and pounded the court. She was hurt badly and would likely miss the state tournament.

Angel sat on the sidelines as she watched her team come in second place in the state championship game. Coach Patrick spoke with Angel after the game. As he placed his hand on top of her head, he told her something she would never forget. He believed the game would have gone a different direction if she would have been healthy enough to play. Her torn knee ligaments made it an impossibility to even try, Angel knew this, but she would never accept it. Coach was a man of very few words, so when he spoke, it was like God himself was speaking through him.

Awaiting her knee reconstruction surgery, she reread the newspaper articles every day, reading how losing one of its star players was detrimental to the team and how inconsolable Angel had been during the injury. Angel was reeling in disappointment, and she was tired, but she knew without a doubt that she had grown up this year.

Making it through her surgery, the physical therapy, and the regret, Angel was working now and had a new boyfriend. Mr. Hammon had switched schools at the end of the year, and Angel didn't care. Things were improving in her life. Though her dad never came around, she tried not to need him anymore. Angel's boyfriend made it a little easier to forget her dad whom she never knew. He treated her well and was a wrestler, so he was also an athlete. Angel couldn't shake the doubts and insecurities of why Mark would want to date her, but she tried to ignore the thoughts. It made it difficult when she was with him and his friends as their girlfriends were much more pretty and never really made Angel feel included in their group.

Angel wanted to look extra nice their date. She moved a little slower since the surgery, but the physical therapist was allowing for her knee to bend more and more each session. She combed through her hair at least a million times, and finally, throwing down the brush and nearly breaking the porcelain sink, she gave up on convincing the mirror she was pretty.

Mark would be there soon.

The date was fun, the movie turned out to be entertaining, and it was nice laughing with Mark. Angel needed laughter since she was feeling more down than normal lately. After the movie, they drove near the river to a place that overlooked the water where the stars glistened perfectly to make the night even more beautiful. Mark asked Angel into the back seat where they could stretch out. His car was nice, roomy enough to drive around most of his wrestling friends. He always felt thankful to have the car and appreciated that his grandparents had been so generous in giving it to him when he got his license. He had added some sporty accessories, and it was something he was proud of. Mark spent a lot of time on his car like most high school boys did.

Making her way to the back seat, she could bend her knee enough to get back there without stretching it too badly. Dodging the beer cans, she found a spot on the floor to place her feet. Mark was still outside opening the trunk searching for something, but Angel couldn't figure out what it could be.

Finally, Mark returned and crawled in next to Angel with a tall can of beer and began to drink it, offering some to Angel.

She tried a sip and then another. In a few short minutes, Mark was opening the third can of the six he brought.

Angel remembered the beautiful shining stars, the smell of stale beer on Mark's breath, and very little more from that evening—only that she was served many beers by the person she was supposed to trust with her heart, and who she tried to make love her and not leave her.

On the way home, this boy she thought she knew pulled over twice to open the door and allow Angel to get sick. His car was much too precious to let it happen inside with his clean seats, dashboard, and floor mats.

Angel found herself back at home. The empty couch that turned into a bed was still a bed, and Larry's things were still resting in the same place they were when he passed away. With her mom still working at the convenience store, it gave Angel time to figure things out.

Terror swept over Angel. The rooms were closing in on her as she rinsed out her mouth and wiped her face. Mark didn't tell her good-bye or see that she made it in the house alright. Flashbacks of the last year bombarded her mind. She felt as if tiny bugs or snakes were crawling over her body. She wasn't a stranger to these creatures. They visited her almost nightly in her dreams. Slowly, Angel made it into the shower, dizzy from alcohol and still tasted her own bile from retching on the side of the road. She couldn't stand the thought of herself. As the water ran down her damaged body, her incision was still bright pink from the repaired ligament that stole her life and stole her reason for living. Everything was truly gone.

Nearly using an entire bar of soap, Angel violently attempted to clean her shame, guilt, worthlessness, and ugliness down the drain. Unsuccessfully accomplishing the impossible, Angel's first tear fell, opening the door to the endless stream to flow with the running water. She dropped onto her back and let the water beat down onto her stomach. Making a tight fist, she one by one, blow by vicious blow, attacked what the surgeon repaired not long ago. Soon, her knee took all the blame as it swelled two sizes bigger. Choking on water as she filled and emptied her mouth, she cried harder and harder. The only words she could speak were, "Daddy, Daddy."

# Chapter 6

# His Daughter

*I'm here, Angel, my daughter. I'm here, and you are beautiful. Not broken. Not damaged, and I love you. Someday, you will know. Your faith will be not of this world. Your story will help the wounded and the meek. I will use your strength to change lives, and your light will shine. I broke the key that you held in your fist, and you will not come home until your race is won.*

Weeks turned into months as Angel's morning sickness turned into a protruding abdomen with a new life growing inside of her. Although her mom wasn't pleased, she had always wanted a grandchild, so much so that it motivated her mom to quit smoking. Angel thought how pleasant it was to not smell smoke seep from under her bedroom door in the mornings as her mom prepared for her many hours of work ahead.

As Angel neared full term, she grew full of so much love for this new life within her. Her regular clothes became smaller and smaller, but just the opposite was true for her heart. She was full of the best love on earth. Mother to child. Even at her young age, Angel created in her mind how much she would care for her baby. These thoughts became her lifeline. Her journal entries shifted from pain to maybe having some purpose. Someone would need her, and someone would love her. She felt scared, but her new love and hope for her child made her fear evaporate. Angel knew Mark wouldn't be back. He never cared for her and never loved her. She knew the truth now—he left and was never going to look back.

Although most of Angel's days were full of dirty looks at school, whispers behind her back, and hours of sneaking into the restroom of her high school to cry, she held onto the hope of what it would feel like to hold her baby in her arms for the first time.

Exiting the restroom, she was thankful for the end of the week. Angel used her sleeves to wipe away her final tears and proceeded to her locker. Negotiating the obstacles of usual glances and daggers of contempt, she opened her locker and gathered what she needed for the weekend. Angel began to hear laughter ensuing two lockers away from her. It was where most of the pretty girls congregated. Jenny and Megan stood pointing and giggling at Angel. Their cheerleading outfits snuggled against their thin and unblemished bodies. Their hair was flowing so long, framing their made-up faces. Angel felt herself become numb and stood frozen, staring into her locker. Hoping they would walk away, Angel pretended to search for her backpack even though it was still on the middle hook where she had left it that morning, just like she did every morning. Somehow, Angel always kept straight As and was a good student. More and more commotion began to drown out the girls' whispers and giggles. Angel clenched her fist and dug her fingernails into the palm of her hand to free the anger from within her.

God has NEVER said anything negative about ME.

Angel's mind drifted to thoughts of what her dad may be doing. Her sensation of numbness continued as the noise around her became muffled. She would give her life to just see her dad right now, and she wondered what a hug from him would feel like. Did he have strong arms? Would he smile at her? One lonely tear streamed from her check and rested itself on the oversized T-shirt covering her growing baby belly.

That nigh Angel rested in her bed, ready to fall asleep and start over again tomorrow. Writing in her journal became more of a countdown to her due date. Soon, she could hold her baby boy. Since finding out that the baby she was carrying was a boy, she was drawing even closer to the life growing inside of her but had yet to see. What would he look like? Would he have a lot of hair? Would he weigh enough? And would he be healthy? Angel began to think about the way those girls laughed at her and the way they looked down at her and made her feel small and insignificant. Through a burst of stinging tears, Angel began to pray. She asked God to help her, pleaded her fear with him and her loneliness, and she confessed to God that her strength was almost gone. She would need His if this baby were to be born to a good mother. Hoping He would listen this time, she pleaded for God to help her ... His daughter. Angel wasn't sure where those words came from within her prayer. She just wanted God to see her and to help her as she pled her case. For the first time, she called herself His daughter to her God. To Angel that felt good, and right now, in her bedroom, that was all she needed.

Looking from her window to the dark sky, a few stars lit up her little corner of the world. She stood up and outstretched her arms toward where she imagined heaven to be. Closing her eyes tightly, she began to feel a sudden tightening of her abdomen that took her breath away. She placed her arms around her stomach and bent over, holding her breath.

"Mom!" Angel hollered, as she opened her mom's bedroom door. Leaving a puddle of liquid in her mom's doorway, she realized this was what her doctor had told her about—her water had just broke. Angel was going to see her baby boy very soon.

# Chapter 7

# Crying Over Spilled Juice

*My daughter, you are feeling the Holy Spirit. I am sending you my strength. I am your Father, and I love you even more than you love your new baby. I hear your prayers, your baby will grow into a boy and into a man, and will become and will always be your pride and joy. This boy will love you like no man could. Your heart will find peace, and you will understand my love. You asked for helping hand—I sent you your first son.*

Angel ultimately survived high school, and each day, as she looked into her son, Nicholas's, eyes, she forgot the pain of childbirth. Those little brown eyes, warm smile, and the sounds of his unique dump truck and race car sounds made her heart sing. Angel found herself doing her everyday tasks well with the help of her mom and a new friend she made in a support group for new young mothers.

Lori became her best friend very quickly; it was easy to see how important she became to Angel, and she didn't feel alone knowing they had so much in common. Lori, a strong, courageous, and loving friend, was an amazing mom whom Angel hoped to be like someday. She had found a real friend, whose pain she helped. Lori did the same for Angel without even trying. She never thought friendship could look and feel so wonderful. Beyond the ongoing nightmares Angel had when Nicholas allowed her to sleep, her life was making a turn for the better. She had faith. Angel felt loved and needed and had a sense of belonging all because of this new little one.

As Angel held Nicholas, she wondered if this was how Jesus loved her. Is this the warmth she felt at night as she rested, as she lay as still as she possibly could? What seemed like a perfect plan for her life when there was always a nagging pull for her heart? No matter how much peace she felt, the way Nicholas's love made her melt with such an enormous purpose, she had a job, her mother was helping her, and her goals of going to college someday, she still couldn't escape the haunting visions she didn't know how to free herself from. Asking God to release her from these negative thoughts became a daily routine. She wanted to be happy and not live in fear as she had done her entire life. Angel started to believe the thoughts that told her there was something wrong with her. Nightmares would intensify at times, and the sensation of the bugs crawling on her and men chasing her and not being able to awaken from them plagued her. The black cloud that would find its comfortable place over her head would rain; other days, the clouds would just lurk over her head. She never felt this darkness go away.

Tucking Nicholas in his crib was Angel's favorite thing to do. After giving him his bath and bottle, she would kiss his soft, lavender-scented face and softly sing him to sleep. Soon, she would get a bath of her own and tuck her worn-out and damaged body to bed. Before even thinking of being able to fall asleep, she asked herself the same questions tonight. Would she be a good enough mother? Would Nicholas always love her? How was she going to make it?

Being a good mother meant making enough money to support her and her little boy. Angel knew she couldn't live with her mom forever, and working as a housekeeper at an insurance building downtown wasn't going to pay the bills. Each evening, she left Nicholas with her mom to clean up messes she felt resembled her own life. A life of feeling unworthy, exhausted, and useless was the garbage she dumped, the toilets she cleaned, and the gum she scraped from under the cafeteria tables in the office. Somehow, she had to find a way to make more money.

After cleaning the insurance building, just like she always had since starting the job, beginning with dumping the garbage in all the cubicles then onto dusting, trying not to knock over the family pictures the employees had decorating their small work areas, Angel stopped to look at the same pictures every night at the same time of night. Keeping herself on task, she wondered what each family member in the pictures was doing. Were they having dinner, playing with their kids, laughing, or snuggling in bed? The end of this night was different from just putting all her cleaning supplies in the janitor closet and driving the same route home. Angel couldn't believe where she found the route leading her to tonight.

Her mom's car was almost out of gas; she has run the car on fumes before. She would do it again, though this trip she wished for the gas vapors left in the tank to not be enough to get her to her destination. As she drew closer to the building, her heart was pounding so strong and fast. Angel saw the billboard of the strip club, the blinking lights of the naked women figures beckoning her to drive closer. Angel was barely of age, but she was going to try to use what was left of her body to buy gas for her mom's car, milk for Nicholas, and hopefully have enough to help pay her portion of the utilities.

Parking under the glow of the blinking breasts, Angel could feel the numbness in her soul and the emptiness of her lonely heart. She could feel the beads of sweaty shame surface over her forehead. Her muscles seemed to barely be enough to start the process of getting out of the car. Angel put bright red lipstick over her lips, blush over her cheeks, and black mascara on her eyelashes, and as she finished spraying more hairspray over her hair, she slid her purse under the seat of her mom's car.

Angel adjusted the high heels meant for feet two sizes smaller than hers, and she opened the car door and placed one heel on the ground and then the other. The rocks layering the parking lot were bumpy, making it difficult to negotiate her steps. Belligerent, drunk shenanigans carried on into the parking lot as she remembered the owner telling her when she called to ask a few questions that amateur nights where their busiest nights. Angel needed money and needed it now so she kept carefully walking toward the door to a place she could earn money with a body that wasn't hers anyway.

Scuffing footsteps began to catch up behind her, first slowly and then speeding up. They caught up to her and then matching her speed, the familiar scent of stale alcohol was in the air. It was a smell she knew all too well from a very young age. It meant her dad was home.

"Hey, you!" the scuffing footsteps behind her said as she felt the sensation of moist breath on the nape of her neck.

Angel ignored the voice, hoping it would go away. In an instant, a tight grip snatched her arm and twisted her body around like a rag doll. Her high heels lost their footing, and she tumbled to the gravel. Her throat began to tighten, but she swore not to cry. Angel's scraped both of her knees, and she could feel that she was harmed. The tight skirt she had on slipped up above her waist, but again, she swore not to cry.

"I was talking to you." A tall, staggering, and drooling man scolded her as he looked down at her.

"Leave me alone," Angel whimpered, trying to get up.

Angel closed her eyes tightly and swore she would not cry. Lifting her head, she looked past the neon breasts, neon legs, and neon bodies of the flashing bar sign and fixed her eyes into the sky. It was a crystal-clear night with stars lining up in their once-in-a-lifetime arrangement. She wondered how God could take handfuls of thousands of these stars, toss them into the night sky, and make them look so brilliant.

Time seemed to stop as in her defeated and threatened state Angel still couldn't feel her body, all she had the strength to do was ask for Jesus.

"What did you say?" the man asked as he kicked up gravel and dust into Angel's face.

Soon, lights and sirens could be heard in the distance. Angel took a small corner of her bikini top and tried to clean her face. The man stood up from over top her and took off running, staggering into the moon lit night.

By this time, more men were exiting the bar to see what the disturbance was outside. Angel looked up from the ground and saw the array of all the different sizes and shapes of the men gathering about as they tripped over one another, obviously overserved. Angel needed to get out of there and to her mom's car. In the distance, she could vaguely hear and see the lights of the police cruiser. She found the strength somehow to get up to her feet, something her mom always taught her—that when you fall, you have to pull yourself up by the bootstraps and keep fighting. Angel made it to her car and exited through the back entrance.

Her injured knees now experiencing penetrating pain to the bone. Her trembling hands were gripping the steering wheel, and she still swore she would not cry. Driving a distance away from that awful place she knew she'd never go back to, she took her jacket and covered herself up as she pulled into the gas station on what was left of fumes in her mom's gas tank.

Angel turned on the dome light, seeing clearly the gas warning light was on. Angel got out onto her hands and bruised knees and reached under each of the seats looking for loose change. A quarter here, a nickel there, anything. Moving to the rear of the car, she thought she saw a dollar bill from the corner of her eye. Quickly reaching for it before it disappeared, Angel took it in her hand. She somehow managed to find almost four dollars—enough to buy a small container of whole milk for Nicholas and enough gas to at least get her home.

Ashamed, embarrassed, and completely discouraged, she entered the gas station and found the restroom where she scrubbed the makeup off her face. Angel leaned her arms onto the sink, and it was then she decided to find a way to change her life and to make something of herself for Nicholas. Could she go to college? Could she get a better job?

As she stared into the mirror, she tried as best as she knew how, but she couldn't stop them … the tears poured down her face like an endless fountain dripping into the germ-infested sink. Drying one tear and then another, she could buy Nicholas's milk and then put enough gas in her mom's car to drive home.

As her mascara-stained face touched her pillow, Angel picked up her journal as quietly as she could as to not awaken her son. With some sense of peace of knowing that Nicholas had milk for the morning, she began to write.

Angel wrote about how Jesus could have been the only saving presence as that man attacked her, she wondered why now? Why did He listen when all her life He hadn't? She couldn't stop her thoughts, and she didn't want to. The only problem was her pen couldn't keep up with them.

*I don't know who I am. I wish I were someone else, someone confident, someone with strength. Please help me. Jesus, come back. I don't want to live anymore. If I died, the pain would finally go away. If I can't die, then Jesus, hold my heart and don't let go ...*

Angel concluded these thoughts with jotting down ideas of attending college. She knew she wanted to help care for people, and maybe she would be good at it.

# Chapter 8

# Telephone Call

*My darling daughter, I will never forsake you.
I have your heart, and when you run from me,
I will wait and always keep you in sight. I will
hold you like the little lamb who was lost and
then found. One day, you will be secure in who
you are you. Don't be afraid or discouraged.
Rather, be strong and courageous. You see ... you
have a fighter's heart, and I am your strength.
Satan's schemes will distort this strength by
using the fears and shame you carry. Those
emotions are not from God.*

Enough time had passed. Nicholas was another year older, and Angel's housekeeping job was stable, though still low paying. Her mom continued to maintain her two jobs, and between the three of them, they made a pretty good team. Angel even began her first general prerequisite for nursing at the local community college. Each day she came to class, she was able to hold her head a little higher. Finding enough long-sleeved shirts to cover the scars from several years ago, she felt on her way to being a new person. Angel even fancied a student in her class named Josh. For some reason, the two of them gravitated toward each other during labs. She would catch him looking in her direction several times during class. Brushing it off, she knew all the other girls in her class (and in the universe, for that matter) were more attractive and better at everything. She made up her mind to stay focused on her class work, raising her son, and finishing school. The only male who meant anything to her was her son, and she loved him with a love that was not of this world.

Another long day of classes transitioned to a long night of cleaning up everyone else's messes. As she busied herself on the two floors of the insurance building, she wished and wondered why the life messes she had made weren't as easy to clean up. Angel smiled at the thought of how simple that would be. Still not knowing where her energy was coming from, she finished her shift and still believed she had some energy left for studying once Nicholas was asleep. Her mom had always told Angel he wanted to see his mommy's face before he went night-night. Unknowingly, this is where Angel's strength and energy came from, her small victories at home.

Nicholas had on his Thomas the Tank Engine pajamas on with built-in feet. As she opened the front door, his angelic voice excitedly repeated the beautiful name, "Mommy." Angel wondered why Nicholas wasn't in his crib yet knowing he may not yet asleep, he should still be ready to close his eyes for the night. Her mom usually made sure he was in bed the same time every night.

Angel scooped up her growing little boy and kissed him with butterfly kisses. Her mom, she heard faintly in the back room, was on the phone. Angel could smell the faint scent of a cigarette. Walking closer to the back of the house, she heard her mom sobbing, trying to keep her tears from Angel. Tears maybe she could hide, but in no way could Angel forget the smell of her mom's cigarettes. Panic struck Angel and worried her as something must have shook her mom to the core for her failed attempt at trying to hide a cigarette.

Nicholas's eyes were getting heavier, and he nuzzled a little closer to Angel's neck. She loved his touch, his skin, and his tender hands. Angel wrapped her arms around him even tighter.

"I love you to the moon and back, Nicky" Angel tucked her miracle into his bed with more butterfly kisses, quickly closing the door to keep whatever cigarette smoke was floating around out of her sons' lungs.

Angel crept down the stairs, trying to listen to her mom's phone call. Hoping her mom was okay, she rounded the corner in time to see her mom hang up the phone.

"Mom, what's wrong?" Angel asked as she reached for her crying mother.

Angel's mom took her by the hands and led her to the living room. Dodging large toys on the floor from Nicholas's creations, the two of them made it to the sofa.

Angel knew it was something serious. Her mom had been smoking, the house was more of a mess than normal, and they were sitting together on the sofa, something life never allowed them to do.

"Angel, it's your dad," Angel's mom trailed off as she began to cry some more.

"My dad?" Angel asked, the sound of those words was foreign to her. Over and over, she attempted to repeat those two words in her mind until they sunk in.

"My dad? My dad? My dad?" Did she even have a dad? At first, Angel became angry at why her mom was upset. She didn't care. Why should she care? Why? She realized that any hope of ever seeing him again may be gone. Her mom continued through her sobs to best describe what happened. His brain was bleeding—that's really all Angel needed to know She was far enough in her nursing classes to know that bleeding in your brain was never good.

"He's at the hospital right now, Angel," her mom continued. "Unconscious. Do you want to go see him?"

Angel picked herself up off the couch.

"Mom, I don't know," Angel screamed into her hands.

Her mouth was dry, and her stomach turned upside down and inside out as she ran to the car. Angel somehow found herself walking through the automatic ER door, feeling the rush of hospital air in her face. The hospital smell made her feel weaker and more helpless.

Nurses and other hospital staff members flew up and down the hallways, saving lives. There was one life just beyond the double doors titled Emergency Room that Angel spent all her days for as long as she could remember wanting to see, and she was losing hope that this one life would ever see her.

She approached the double doors that led to her dying dad. Nearly running into them, she realized they weren't opening. Looking around, no one was there. Where had all the busy-body nurses gone? Was everyone deaf? She proceeded to pound on the glass. There was only a waiting room to her back that was full of alive patients, alive dads.

"I want my dad!" Angel screamed as she continued to pound on the glass. Angel didn't know where this rage was coming from. She just slammed her fists on the glass doors over and over until someone saw her or heard her.

She rested her head on the sharp edge of the glass door,

and at the same time, she felt a soft hand on the small of her back. Startled, Angel turned around slowly and saw a small lady standing before her. She was strong in stature with short brown hair, looking to be in her fifties, with kindness filling her gentle hazel eyes. Beyond her blue scrub top, Angel felt a warm presence surround them both that seemed to be more than this nurse's soft touch and sincere care. Soon, the nurse took Angel away from the glass doors and placed her hands close to her body in hopes of making Angel feel safe. She didn't know what was happening. She was trusting this stranger and then began to cry onto her shoulder. She could see through blurred vision this nurse's name badge read Deb. Soon, Deb had Angel's tears dried, and she led her to room twelve, the room where her dad laid lifeless. Deb squeezed Angel's hands one last time as she tried to let Angel go. Angel had such a grip on Deb's that she didn't want to let go. Angel felt all alone, knowing that through the door was her dad. He was more of a stranger to her than the nurse who dried her tears and held her hands.

Angel pried her fingers apart from Deb's, and as she walked into her dad's room, Deb stood waiting for her outside. Angel was soon bombarded with beeps and dings and sounds of the ventilator and cardiac monitor as well as many nurses who weren't Deb. The coldness of this room made Angel's heart beat slower and her blood run cold. No one said a word. Angel neared the bed her dad was going to die in. She still couldn't see his face. His legs were an outline under the sheets and blankets. If Angel looked close enough, she could see her dad's ten toes. This may be the closest she'd ever been to the man who gave her earthly life.

She lifted her hand and touched her dad's arm, raised her head, and saw his face. Eyes closed, bleeding from both ears, with a tube in his mouth leading down his throat, he was attached to the machine that was breathing for him.

Angel then touched his hair. Surprisingly, she now knew where her natural curls came from. Following down, she never left his touch, and as she reached his hand, she also now new where her strong and hardworking hands came from. Angel took a hold of her dad's hand and began to cry tears that she hadn't felt before. Her stomach started to twist, and she vomited all over herself. Trying hard to not get her dad dirty, she used her shirt to clean her mess. By this time, nurses were trying to hurry Angel's visit, but she wasn't going to let go of her dad's hand, and it would take an army to get her to do so. Angel opened her purse with her free hand and dug through the mess of papers, a few dollar bills, and her lip balm to find the latest photograph of Nicholas.

Angel took the picture of her boy in one hand and the corner of her dad's sheet in the other hand. As she dried the blood from his ears, she told her dad there was someone he had to meet and that he couldn't die. Angel folded the picture of her son and placed it in her dad's hand, closed his fist tightly, and left the room where her dad's machines that kept him breathing and his heart beating would cease soon.

Angel was sick and could barely walk as she vomited yet again into the nearest restroom. Opening the door, she had never felt so empty, so alone, so abandoned. Angel asked herself in the midst of all the chaos and pain what she had to do to hold onto God's grace. Why did He seem to always allow such ache in her heart? Angel pleaded quietly to God on that sterile restroom floor less than two rooms away from the only man she ever needed love from. He was going to die, and her glimpse of hope now has burned out. Curling up into a fetal position, Angel began to believe herself to be truly lost. She had nothing. How could she be a mother worthy of her little boy? Her own dad didn't love her, and yet, she had to find the strength to carry on without ever looking over her shoulder again, hoping he would be there. She would never look at the phone hoping he would call and never drive hoping one of the cars she saw on the road was him.

The only confidence she had was hidden deep in her soul. Searching with everything she had left, she was able to get to her feet. It was this confidence that led her to the hospital doors and back home to her son.

# Chapter 9

# A Fight outside the Octagon

*I hear your prayers. I know you're lost and
scared. Hold fast. Your journey will set you free.
I sent you Deb.*

Angel couldn't find sleep very well since losing her dad,
the man whom she never remembered feeling hugged by
and never remembered saying he loved her. She pressed on
with classes, raising her son, and working at the insurance
building. Her ugliness scarred her for life. Her mind was her
worst enemy, believing something was always going to be
wrong with her.

She couldn't comfortably go anywhere. She felt inadequate,
looking at couples together. Pretty girls made her feel even
more worthless. Angel only wished she could have been
prettier. Maybe things would have been different. Avoiding
the gaze of men became her reality. She became sweaty and
nauseated, and numbness swept over her body. Something
was wrong. She didn't understand but accepted it as she
learned to accept everything else.

There was another trip to the grocery store today for a
few more items. Angel was there yesterday, but she seemed

to always forget something. Moving slowly on this another Saturday morning with Nicholas playing with his toys, she knew he would be upset to go with her. Throwing clothes on Nicholas and putting her hair up in a ponytail, they began their adventure. Angel did her best at calming Nicholas. Bringing a bag of his toys didn't seem to be enough entertainment to keep him from making his feelings of disappointment known.

"It won't take that long, honey," Angel said convincingly.

Securing Nicholas on her hip as she had done a million times, she speed walked into the store for the three items she forgot yesterday. Pull-ups, bananas, and juice. She was surprised to see the store wasn't that busy as she entered, always impressed with the displays of perfect fruits and vegetables that Angel wished she could afford. The canned options weren't the same, but right now, they would have to do. All the happy people smiling with their carts as she passed them making her way with Nick bouncing on her hip, she was on a mission to not have to use a cart and pick up her things.

"Juice first," Angel mumbled as she made plans for her quick departure from the store.

She slowed her walk as she approached the plethora of choices. One thing that made no sense was why there had to be so many choices. She picked up the usual white grape juice that was Nicholas's favorite. Angel was always pleased at how well she could juggle her grocery items avoiding using a cart. Using a cart equaled spending more money than she had. She dreamed of one day using a grocery cart every trip to the grocery store, even if she only needed one item. The best part would be that she wouldn't have to hide the toilet paper she stole from the community college restroom in her backpack anymore. One day, she would pay her student loans off, maybe find a long-lasting love, and maybe have more kids.

Angel often let her mind wander during random times of the day. This grocery store visit was one of those random times. It kept her from feeling uncomfortable with all the people spending their money, laughing, and carrying on with their significant others and friends. Angel startled herself, letting the large glass door from the array of juice selections slam shut and wondering how long she had been day dreaming as Nicholas wriggled happily grunting funny words while pointing out bright donut and bakery displays. Free cookies for the kids was probably the most fun Nick could have on the various trips they had to take to the store.

Becoming more excited, knowing it was almost time for his cookie, Nicholas giggled as the two made their way closer to the free samples. On approaching the choices of cookies, Angel's mood changed from happiness and contentment with her son to an unexpected uncomfortable sense of a presence near her that was making her feel uneasy. Her heart was beginning to race as found herself in the next aisle, trying to hurry to the checkouts.

Making her way around the corner to the checkouts, she suddenly came face to face with a man who looked familiar—not the "old friend" kind of way but in a "seeing a ghost kind of way". As soon as Angel realized who it was, she lost her grip on the juice, shattering the plastic bottle as it fell to the grocery store floor of aisle eight. Standing in a puddle of white grape juice and numb head to toe, she saw that the man who scared her so was Mr. Hammon. Flashes of high school hijacked her brain and seeing the oak tree that never helped her, she felt the blades of grass on her back and smelled the nauseating cologne that stained her body as he damaged her beauty. Angel held Nicholas close as they sprinted from the store as if they were running from a fire. Panting and gasping for air she reached the car, Nicholas was crying from being jostled in such a manner. Gently, Angel tried as best as she could to put him in his car seat. Angel sat in the driver's seat with her head resting on the steering wheel, not understanding why she uttered the words, "Mr. Hammon sexually abused me".

Angel felt free. Maybe that was what had been wrong with her—all her pain she couldn't explain, her grief, and her feelings of shame. She hadn't seen Mr. Hammon in years, but she always had a nagging finger pointing at herself that she had something off about her. Was this it? Was she abused?

In the weeks to follow, Angel knew she had to face this and not run away. This had to be a part of her journey to being a better mom and a successful healthcare provider and to pave her path to true freedom. As easy as it may seem to ignore her pain and not see what was on the other side, it would ultimately only make things worse to ignore the truth. She was about to begin the biggest fight of her life. Somehow, the word "abuse", as it bounced around in her brain, gave her a reason and an answer to the unanswered questions that she didn't know existed. Was Jesus going to help her?

Angel had to keep all strength she could, stay motivated, and not waiver on her mission. After seeing her perpetrator again, she held onto the hope that maybe she would make it. She wasn't the vulnerable, weak, and easy victim anymore. She would be a survivor.

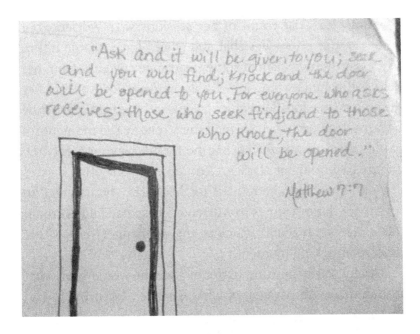

"Ask and it will be given to you; seek and you will find; knock and the door will be opened to you. For everyone who asks receives; those who seek find; and to those who knock, the door will be opened."

Matthew 7:7

After her own pep talk came the urgency of revenge, which simmered to a slow boil with each visit to her counselor, Adriene. The steady boil came to a rolling boil so intense that the pot was overflowing from within her. She learned that the statute of limitations had passed and that criminal charges weren't an option. She would never forget hearing those words spoken by the tall, well-built, and kind police detective who seemed to empathize with her. Even he appeared disappointed in the law that he proudly stood behind.

Angel had a suspicion this seasoned detective wasn't the only one in the department who had to try to keep personal feelings away from the job.

Adriene, Angel's counselor, became a close ally. Adriene's compassion, sensitivity, and the way she let Angel be herself allowed a bond to form, a deep trust was where she found her validation.

Angel had lost count of her sessions with Adriene, but what she did know was that she would have a large bill to pay, even though she had some insurance coverage from her near full-time cleaning job. Today, as Angel drove from her nursing class, she allowed her fatigue get the best of her. She became discouraged. It seemed the strength and momentum going forward was nowhere to be found. Having barely the energy to attend her classes, clean up everyone else's messes at work, and have enough left for Nicholas, she now had to reveal her darkest times to Adriene. These had laid dormant like a disease, ready to attack at any moment. This was that disease-attacking moment.

Angel was beginning to doubt that she would have what it took to slay the dragon of what has been torturing her all these years.

Angel walked through the building doors that led to Adriene's office for yet another session, which had proven to her salvation right now. Taking in the familiar scent of the office building air, which always seemed to have its own unique scent, Angel once again chose the elevator rather than the stairs as they accommodated her tired body much better. Adriene's office was comfortable. There were a lot of positive signs with encouraging words. There were a few that always caught her eyes: *"Learn from Yesterday, Live for Today, Hope for Tomorrow"* and *"She decided to star to live the life She Imagined"*.

"If only it were that easy," Angel would sit there thinking as she waited for Adriene to open her office door to welcome her in. Adriene carried herself so confidently. Her healing eyes made it easy to open up to her, and she was tall and very beautiful. Her kindness reminded her of the nurse who Angel met as her dad lay lifeless in the hospital.

Even now, as many times as she came in to see Adriene, Angel still couldn't wrap her head around why Adriene wanted to help her. Angel's feelings of not getting better fast enough and being a lost cause won the battle for her thoughts most days. She knew Adriene cared because she saw Adriene cry during some of their sessions.

The elevator was as it had been all the other visits—quiet, cold, and small. Usually Angel was the only occupant, but today, there was a variety of people. A few women joined Angel for the swift ride to the fourth floor where many small businesses made their start. Tucked at the end of the hall, in the corner, was the entrance to Adriene's office. A cozy gathering of chairs lined the walls with a few magazines on the end tables to distract the clients from their own misery. Not being too interested in magazines, Angel deeper into her pit of not ever feeling good enough. Angel took her usual seat after signing in with Elaine, a happy and always-smiling office manager who somehow made Angel feel glad she was there.

The same scratches were still lining the right armrest of the wooden padded waiting room chair. Angel could recognize this chair anywhere since she had spent so much time in it, waiting to heal her what seemed to be impossible brain.

Adriene began the session explaining the process of EMDR. It was a way to make traumatic events not so powerful. Eye movement desensitization and reprocessing therapy, Adriene explained, is a proven treatment for victims of trauma. Placing two plastic oval-shaped objects into Angel's palms would serve as a piece to the process. Adriene continued to explain the procedure, telling Angel the two plastic ovals in her palms would alternate small vibrations from one closed palm to the other while memories of Angel's abuse, her perpetrator, and the feelings of loss concerning her dad were triggered from the parts of her brain that were locked so tightly in hopes of bringing them to light and taking some of the pain, hurt, shame, and despair away.

Today would be the day Angel would start stopping at the flower shop for bouquets of flowers after her sessions. The pure and utter exhaustion was unexplainable. Angel believed the only thing positive and blessed in these moments after the next several meetings with Adriene were flowers.

It was during this phase of her life that she was thankful for the perseverance and determination she knew came from Coach Patrick. He who always thought Angel had potential. Angel could begin to hear her own voice. It had a sound of its own. New strength was forming, and it felt new and so unfamiliar. Though not understanding still why God would have such a mess of a woman be a mother, Angel often became triggered with flashbacks of the abuse, her dad's death, and Larry's frail body withering to skin and bones in her living room.

For the first time, Angel honestly with her entire heart wondered if a man would ever want to be with her and think she was enough. Would she be loved? Would she ever feel like a princess? After all her mistakes? After all of her regrets? She feared she would chase her future prince away.

There was still a focus deep within Angel in wanting to finish nursing school. Even with all her doubts about her life, questions of why, and all of her should haves, she was nearing the end of her last semester. She had persevered, had fought the fight of her life, and didn't even know it.

The fatigue overshadowed her progress much of the time, becoming too much to bear at times. The guilt of being tired and distracted to play with Nicholas haunted her nightly. Thoughts of suicide, her pain, the EMDR treatments, and being triggered by memories were resurfacing at unexpected times and with a vengeance. Adriene was confident the storm would calm in time.

Angel was fearful of cutting again. Her clinical assignments were starting at the hospital, and she didn't want anyone to see the marks. Instead of mutilating her body on the outside, she starved herself on the inside. Driving to school during one of her last mornings of the semester, she set a record for herself, thirty-six hours without food. She was weak and had a severe headache but mustered up a smile as she stared at the picture of Nicholas she wedged in her mom's dashboard of her car a few weeks ago. It was a reminder to Angel that she must live to see him grow and be a man.

This small picture of a young boy with the toothless grin and his sweet little shoes certainly rescued her from the brink, none so real and so saving, she recalled, as she remembered finished her clinic day the week before. She was helplessly tired walking to her car that day, wondering why her Jesus couldn't heal all the sick she cared for on that day. Finishing her last patient's care, Angel could see perfectly the parking ramp from the fifth floor critical care unit. On that specific day, she made her plans to jump. Angel looked at her patient and looked at the parking ramp. She begged silently for Jesus to allow her to trade places with the middle-aged woman who experienced a massive heart attack and remained unresponsive. Cleaning her patient up, Angel gently cleansed around her patient's intubation tubing, seeing her dad's flashing lights and monitors in the back of her mind the entire time. Angel wiped her own face on her scrubs, so the patient's family would not see her tears. They were all gathering together, holding hands in the hall where they longed for even an ounce of hope that Angel couldn't provide.

Giving God an ultimatum, Angel would jump today if He wouldn't allow her to trade places with this woman who lay waiting for her heart to beat on its own again.

As Angel finished her charting that day, she kept an eye on the main monitors at the nurse's desk, concentrating on room 534, her patient. There was still no change. Angel was still breathing, believing full well that God didn't do as she asked and chose to let this woman suffer and her family suffer for no reason.

It all rushed in like a murder of crows attacking its prey. Angel let a tear fall on her steering wheel as she continued to remember that day, hearing through her tears the faint sound of music filtering through her speakers. Angel hadn't realized she already started the car. The lyrics were like God's soft touch upon her life that was getting ready to call it quits. The lyrics made it a battle to match the fierceness of her tears.

*How many times have you heard me cry out*
*"God please take this"?*
*How many times have you given me strength to*
*Just keep breathing?*
*Oh I need you*
*God, I need you now.*

*Songwriters: Christa Nichole Wells/Luke Harry Sheets/Tiffany Arbuckle Lee "Need You Now" by Plumb*

All Angel was supposed to do was to keep breathing—that's it. She could do that. She heard the still-small voice of

God and looked at the small hands and feet of the wallet-sized picture of her boy tucked behind the speedometer.

Hiding near the bottom of her backpack under more stolen rolls of toilet paper from the hospital restrooms was a class assignment she saved for reasons she now understood. Angel had a fascination and sincere interest in the unit the class studied on hospice. She was obsessed with it, to say the least, and Angel felt her gift may rest on her ability to focus on caring for the terminally ill patients—easing their pain and making them as comfortable as they could be emotionally and spiritually was what she felt she could do.

The assignment, when given, was very annoying and inappropriate to all of Angel's classmates when the professor assigned it. She could hear the snide remarks, complaints, and hysterics, but Angel embraced the task of writing her own obituary.

"This would be easy," Angel remembered whispering above her peers as they complained. Unsure why she kept it, she unfolded the piece of notebook paper that held the words that highlighted and described the end of her life.

Angel began to read it aloud after making the pivotal decision to keep breathing ...

*Angel Nicole Jordan died September 1, 2015, at her home. She succumbed to the ravages of the pain of Post-Traumatic Stress Disorder to which she fought during entire life and was unable to find peace here. She was born on April 24.. Passing before her were her grandmother, her father, and her stepfather. Survivors include her son, Nicholas, and her mother.*

*Angel will be remembered for her love of Jesus, her love of her son, and the passionate way she cared for her friends. She wished for everyone to have peace in their lives even if she didn't. Angel died a fighter, and God is lucky to have her in His kingdom, where she will not be in secret pain any longer.*

*In lieu of flowers, donations can be made to a local suicide-prevention group or suicide hotline.*

Hearing her own words and her own voice as she read aloud the story of her death, Angel believed she had to be a survivor. She had come too far not to. Before putting the car in drive, she tore up her obituary into small pieces, stepped out of her car, climbed up on and stood high up on the cement wall of the fifth floor parking ramp where she was to jump only minutes ago, to her death. She looked down and saw the cars and people who were like scurrying ants rushing here and there but never really getting anywhere.

Without hesitating, she threw the handful of pieces of paper describing her death up into the air over the wall.

She never wanted to remember how she almost took a mother from a son, a daughter from her mother, and a caregiver from her patients.

# CHAPTER 10

# ALIVE

*I am at work, my daughter. When you think I'm distant, your God is working the hardest. Angel, your race will be won. Your faith, obedience, and love will be blessed. With Me, all things are possible. The challenges and troubles you aren't immune from. You will be faced with choices, and your walk toward eternity and our relationship will grow amidst the world and its destruction.*

With each bouquet of bright beautiful flowers, week by week, month by month, Angel began to see her worth. She became sick with the idea of ever hurting herself again. The old rusted knife resting beneath old pictures and her son's artwork in the drawer of her nightstand was now resting beneath garbage in the garbage can of her kitchen where it belonged.

The journal entries in the tattered journal her grandmother gave her so many years ago changed. The entries became optimistic. She was closer to Jesus and could feel how much her true Father in heaven loved her. He was a Father who would never forsake her or leave her, a Father who kept His promises.

Angel prayed one last prayer in her grandma's journal. She had only a small amount of empty space left in the journal that held safely onto the words from her heart and soul for so long. Sprinkled in here were her most intimate talks with God. In this last prayer that this journal would contain, she prayed her hopes and dreams, her desires, and her ache for two more sons who would, like Nicholas, be her miracles. She wrote about thankfulness for her mom, her son, Nicholas, and her nursing career she would embark on soon, and she dreamed of helping other young women and anyone else who faced battles. She wanted to do whatever God called her to do. Angel knew her times of making mistakes, poor choices, and having regrets weren't over, but she asked for the Lord's forgiveness and His strength to give her courage to follow His will for her life.

Angel closed the journal and placed it over her heart as she stood up. Walking taller, she looked in the mirror, and for the first time in her life, she saw herself in the reflection staring back at her.

# AFTERWORD

In the months to follow, Angel used the newfound, God-given strength she saw in her eyes, used her passion, and used the validation she gained from Adriene to confront her perpetrator, Mr. Hammon.

Though she knew the other girls he victimized weren't willing to come along side of her and share their stories, even after she called and visited them personally many times, it wasn't the right time for them. She would have to do this on her own. The statute of limitations was working against her, and legally, she had no chance at criminal charges. Angel had to make her voice heard by the one person that attempted to steal it from her.

Ultimately, Angel offered him forgiveness. She embraced the opportunity to grow from being a victim into being a survivor with or without prosecution. Giving all the glory to God, she knew she would never forget what happened. However, the ripple effect this trauma has caused would no longer keep her in its wake.

"The Lord is my light and my salvation — whom shall I fear?"

Psalm 27:1

CPSIA information can be obtained
at www.ICGtesting.com
Printed in the USA
BVOW04s0452070517
483420BV00001B/7/P